WILLIAM SEABROOK

Astounding Secrets of the Devil-Worshippers' Mystic Love Cult

Revealing the Intimate Details of Aleister
Crowley's Unholy Rites, His Power
Over Women Whom He Branded and
Enslaved, His Drug Orgies, His Poetry
and Mysticisms, His Startling Adventures
Around the Globe as
"the Beast of the Apocalypse"

THIS IS A SNUGGLY BOOK

ISBN: 978-1-64525-106-4

The present text is based on that which was originally serialized in 1923; numerous amendments, however, have been made where obvious errors existed.

Astounding Secrets
of the Devil-Worshippers'
Mystic Love Cult

William Buehler Seabrook (1884–1945) was an American journalist and explorer whose lifelong fascination with the occult, and various other interests, took him across the globe, where he studied magic rituals, trained as a witch doctor, and according to his own account, ate human flesh. He began his career as a reporter for the *Augusta Chronicle*, and subsequently worked at *The New York Times* and wrote for various newspapers and magazines, including *Cosmopolitan* and *Vanity Fair*. His books include *The Magic Island* (1929), *Jungle Ways* (1930), and *Asylum* (1935).

Astounding Secrets
of the Devil-Worshippers'
Mystic Love Cult

BEAST or poet? Monster or moralist? Charlatan or magician? Genius or madman?

These are the questions Europe has been asking for more than ten years about Aleister Crowley, the most complex characters in the modern world, and one of the most extraordinary in human history.

You will read of a man—

Who has won fame by sublimely beautiful religious poetry, yet has committed blasphemies and sacrileges such as the world has never known.

Who has reveled in orgies that astonished Paris, yet has sat motionless for months as a naked yogi, begging his rice under the hot sun of India.

Who has steeped himself in hasheesh and opium, yet has never become enslaved by them, and accomplished a prodigious volume of literary work.

Who has killed lions and climbed mountains, crossed the Sahara, penetrated to the interior of China where no white man ever went before, yet who has whipped and branded English and American girls who came under his power as slaves were whipped and branded by their masters in ages past.

And his is only the beginning of this "double" character. He is the supreme head of a mystical cult which includes the modern "Devil-Worshippers," a revival of the ancient Rosicrucian Order, Egyptian Masonry and Black Magick, whose ramifications reach Paris, London, New York, Detroit, Chicago and other American cities.

He believes that he is the incarnation of "The Beast of the Apocalypse."

His creed is, "Do what thou wilt shall be the whole of the law." He has just written a new book called *The Diary of a Drug Fiend*, which is the sensation of London. He is now living in Cefalu, Sicily, in an "Abbey," surrounded by his "high priestesses," teaching his doctrines, practicing his strange rites, as he formerly practiced them here in America.

The following chapters will contain the intimate revelation of this astounding character by the writer, who knew and studied Aleister Crowley most closely during the four years of his activities in America and who has kept in close touch with his doings since. They constitute an authentic and authoritative record, backed by indisputable photographs, documents and letters.

CHAPTER I.

ALEISTER CROWLEY already notoriously famous in England, Europe and the Orient—called by his friends and enemies everything from "immortal genius" to "inhuman monster"—arrived in America from nobody knows where.

He may have come from a cell in some Chinese Buddhist monastery—from a scholarly library in London—or an opium dive in Montmarte.

They were all equally his "home."

I just got a wireless message from him dated Cefalu, Sicily, the beautiful spot on the Mediterranean where he founded the "Abbey of Thelema," in which he is the "high priest," directing the secret rites and orgies which still go on, and which I shall later describe. From London come daily newspapers with accounts of the latest sensation he has created in the British capital as the author of a book entitled *The Diary of a Drug Fiend*.

As I am writing these lines the American daily newspapers are carrying reports from Detroit, telling of the "Ryerson scandal" which has just cropped up anew as the result of the "Love Temple" which Crowley founded in that city when he first came to America. He came well armed with impressive introductions. One of them was from Evarard Feilding, second son of Lord Denleigh, secretary for the British Society of Physical Research.

It was addressed to Dr. Hereward Carrington, America's most celebrated scientific student of psychic phenomenon. It said:

"This will introduce to you Aleister Crowley, poet, mystic, mountain climber, big game hunter and general lunatic."

From other sources Carrington had heard that Crowley was the secret ruler of s strange mystical cult, whose lodges and "temples" circled the entire globe, from Egypt and Asia to the drawing rooms of Paris, London, Berlin, New York and other American cities.

He had heard that Crowley was the head of that strange modern survival of the

Middle Ages, "The Devil-Worshippers;" that he was an adept in the dreadful "black magic" of the Orient, and that he possessed powers wielded by no other living man.

After years of careful personal investigation Dr. Carrington, whose opinions stand for cold, scientific precision, said to me: "Whatever else Aleister Crowley may be, I am convinced that he is one of the greatest mystics the world has ever known, and that he probably knows more than any other white man of the secrets of eastern magic."

Today I am inclined to agree with Dr. Carrington, but it makes me smile now to think how different was the impression I got of Aleister Crowley when we first met—four years ago—in a party at the Metropolitan opera.

Crowley appeared during the first entre-act intermission. The first impression was of a punctiliously correct Britisher in conventional evening clothes—a big man, of heavily athletic build, who looked as if he had spent most of his life outdoors. But the conventionality was only on the surface. On presentation to each member of the party, instead of murmuring the usual "How do you do?" or its equivalent, he said:

"DO WHAT THOU WILT SHALL BE THE WHOLE OF THE LAW."

And thereafter, for the entire evening, he sat like an incarnation of the Buddha, staring straight before him, saying nothing at all. The women of the party, I noticed, seemed strangely fascinated by this man—a fascination mingled with a sort of repulsion and fear. Their eyes were on him more than on the stage. He paid no more heed to them than if they hadn't been present. At the end of the evening he said:

"EVERY MAN AND WOMAN IS A STAR."

He said it precisely as you would say "Goodnight," or "It has been a pleasure to meet you," and quietly took his departure.

At this moment, as I said, he is the sensation of London. The newspapers are carrying seven-column headlines about Aleister Crowley on their front pages. *His Diary of a Drug Fiend,* published by a leading London house, has become the center of a raging storm. Some critics have denounced it as "unspeakably wicked" and cried, "Burn the book—and the man!" Others call it a work of sheer genius that "will rank with De Quincey's classical *Confessions of an Opium Eater.*"

And Lea, "The Dead Soul," helped him! "The Dead Soul" when I first met her. "The Scarlet Woman" now! She is not the kind of "Scarlet Woman" you may be thinking of. She is Crowley's—body and soul—and will be faithful to him, I think, until death. And it was she who wrote, in laborious longhand, from his dictation, the novel which is the "raging furor" now in London.

How Crowley changed this girl from "The Dead Soul" into "The Scarlet Woman" recalls my first amazing experience with the real Crowley—an experience in which I participated only as a witness, but which left a more indelible impression on my brain than the most vivid and fantastic novel I have ever read.

It began in Crowley's New York Studio, then at No. 1 University Place, just off Washington Square. Imagine an immense room hung with Oriental tapestries, enormous divans on the floor covered with dull cloth-of-gold, eastern images and idols and statues everywhere—some exquisitely beautiful, some hideous beyond belief. Chairs, tables, modern furniture, too, and bookcases running up to the high ceiling.

Imagine a cosmopolitan gathering of a dozen men and women, invited by Crowley, "for after-dinner coffee and an evening of conversation." Imagine Crowley himself, in a coat and trousers, made in pajama style of a very heavy corded silk, swathing him in black, somber as a priest, brewing coffee, "a la Turcque," in a big Persian copper contrivance something like a samovar, beneath which flickered a bluish flame.

That night Crowley was brilliant, witty, talkative. The conversation ranged from elephant hunting to the sonnets of Shakespeare, to Fifth Avenue fashions and the latest experiment of free verse.

The only person who did not join in the general talk was a girl, or, rather, a woman, for she was probably between twenty-five and thirty, named Lea Hirsig, pretty, but dressed with the utmost quietness and dignity, with a face that seemed a bit sad, a bit disdainful, thoroughly uninterested and detached. I learned afterward that she was a teacher in a children's school.

I do not know whether Crowley had been watching her or not. Certainly her glances had not been markedly fixed on him. But suddenly, during a lull in the talk, he addressed her direct.

"Does nothing interest you, then?" he asked, as if at the end of an exchange of confidences rather than the beginning.

"I'm afraid not," she replied in a monotone. "I am a dead soul——"

Before she had completed whatever else she was going to say, a remarkable change came over Crowley. I was watching his face, and it became, as you have seen the faces of actors become, the face of a man I had never seen before. I do not mean anything necessarily supernatural, but a kind of power blazed from it, as you have seen power blaze from a previously expressionless face in sudden intense excitement. And the eyes, instead of focusing to a converged point, as in normal vision, seemed to stare straight ahead of them, as in separate parallel lines.

"You have spoken," he interrupted, and, curiously enough, his voice was a monotone like her own. "You have spoken, but I am Baphomet, and by my power your dead soul shall wake. You are Lea, the Dead Soul. You shall become Lea, the Scarlet Woman!"

Her answer came like a dash of cold water in the tense silence.

"Mr. Crowley—I believe that is your name—you are absurd. You have no power over me of any kind. I am not interested in you or your absurd pretensions."

Crowley was now standing, looking down at her. As she spoke he moved a step or two further back, stretched out his arms, and began to recite a formula in some curious Hindu dialect. It lasted less than a minute. Neither she nor any of us there understood the meaning of a single syllable. It sounded like an invocation and a command.

Not another word did he speak to her the entire evening. So far as I know he did not look at her again. An hour passed. The guests, including myself, left about midnight—all except Lea.

Without a word to Crowley and without a word of explanation to anybody, like a woman sitting in the waiting room of a railway station—she simply stayed.

Would she have stayed if she had known the fate in store for her? As I read the letters she has sent me since—which she is still sending me—I am compelled to believe that she would.

Four days later I went back one afternoon to see Crowley. I was drawn by an irresistible curiosity. I did not believe in magic, particularly not in Crowley's kind, and I'm not sure that I yet do, though Dr. Carrington and Somerset Maugham (who wrote a book about Crowley's magic) and many other authorities, better qualified than I, agree that this man was and is possessed of powers for which no rational explanation has yet been found. You can interpret the events as you please, calling it hypnotism, charlatanism, animal magnetism, as you like.

I shall merely resound them. They are extraordinary enough in themselves.

Crowley's big studio was on the main floor, first door in the hall to the right. The street door was opened by a porter. I knocked at Crowley's own door. His voice said, "Who is it?" I told him. The voice said, "Come in."

The door yielded to the simple turn of the knob. You have heard people say they "could hardly believe the evidence of their own eyes." The phrase doesn't begin to describe my amazement. You would find it difficult to believe now—this thing that I am going to tell you—except that the extraordinary thing is a matter of record, with first-hand evidence and documentary proofs which can be produced—known to at least a hundred reputable people in New York beside myself.

Lea, the "Dead Soul," was kneeling in the center of a chalked circle, in the middle of the floor. She was bare-footed, like a penitent nun, clad only in a loose robe drawn back over her shoulders, and Aleister Crowley was bending over her—burning magical symbols on her chest with the point of a heated dagger!

Why didn't I interfere? Why didn't I call for the police? I can explain in a few sentences. The big windows of the apartment gaze directly on the corner of Washington Square. People were passing continually. Just outside the unlocked door was the hall, with the porter on duty. Other people could be heard moving in the house. The girl was not bound, not held in any physical way. If she had wanted the scene interfered with she could have stopped it by raising her voice—once.

I looked at her face. She was not drugged. She was not in a stupor. She was obviously in pain. But it was equally obvious that she was—where she wanted to be. An amazing and unheard-of thing in such surroundings—in the New York of the twentieth century. But there it was. And it was her affair and his. And on her face, in addition to the pain, was written—a sort of spiritual ecstasy that you see in old paintings of martyred saints. I haven't seen many happy faces in this world. I did not interfere.

As for Aleister Crowley, he was calm and matter-of-fact as if I had dropped in and found him engaged in his usual occupation of writing. "I shall be finished in about ten minutes more," he said, "and then, if you wish—with the lady's permission, while she rests—we'll have a game of chess."

I sat down and watched. As carefully and gently as a surgeon, he continued the amazing operation—of branding a free woman with a heated dagger point, branding her with her own consent, free-will and co-operation.

He had almost finished tracing a double circle about three inches in diameter, and in the center of this he was now tracing a magical symbol shaped something like a cross.

The girl must have suffered intense pain, but she did not make a single murmur until it was finished. Then, with his help, she got to her feet and retired to an adjoining room.

I don't remember much about the chess game that followed, except that Crowley gave me a knight and rook and beat me with ease. He was imperturbably calm and correct—the Englishman about his own affairs in his own house—and though I wanted to ask a thousand questions I asked none.

I remember that at the end of an hour Lea emerged, calm, smiling, apparently perfectly contented with life; talked interestingly on more or less ordinary subjects, and said when I left, as if her permanent union with Crowley was a matter of course:

"I hope you'll drop in often to see us again."

I did see them "often again" over a period of more than three years. They have never been separated—they are not separated now.

Of how Aleister Crowley completely succeeded in awakening Lea, "The Dead Soul" with the aid of his magical formulas—and a dog-whip—of how he enshrined he as "The Scarlet Woman," the new high priestess of his secret cult, which they are practicing today in Sicily—and of his amazing battle with Leon Kennedy, Dutch artist and mystic, to gain control of the "spirit" of a beautiful red-haired girl named "Kitty Reilly"—I shall tell you in the next chapter.

CHAPTER II.

L AST week I told you how Aleister Crowley—either by black magic or by the force of his amazing personality, whichever you choose to believe—conquered Lea Hirsig, "The Dead Soul." and of how he began the process of transforming her into "The Scarlet Woman."

Since then I had a letter from Lea—dated London—but before telling you what it contained, I want to explain what Crowley meant by his phrase "Scarlet Woman" which keeps bobbing up again and again in his mystical writings.

In current language, it means simply "bad woman," but it was not so that Crowley used it. The phrase is borrowed from the Bible, where it first occurs as "The Scarlet Woman of Babylon"; it was used by the old prophets as the symbol of Paganism. And

Crowley, whose cult was partly a revival of Pagan ceremonies and mysteries, wanted to make Lea his new high priestess.

Lea's family and friends believed that Crowley, with this girl in his clutches, would "destroy her, body and soul," and then cast her aside. But life has a curious way of providing unexpected denouements, and Crowley himself was such a baffling mixture of good and evil that it was never safe to predict his actions.

I was not greatly surprised, therefore, at the contents of Lea's letter, just received from London.

"I am happier than I ever dared to hope," she writes. "We are resting after work. It is good to work, and it is good to rest after work well done. I have written in longhand from A.C.'s dictation more than 150,000 words in a little less than a month on his new novel (this is the novel that is making a bigger sensation in England today than *Jurgen* made in America and presently we are returning to Cefalu."

With this letter before me, I am thinking back to the first months of Lea's association with Crowley in New York and of the ordeals she went through to achieve her "happiness." I saw them intimately and often in those days. I was interested—tremendously—in the extraordinary drama their life presented. And I am thinking now of the beautiful things that Crowley said to her and of the appalling and dreadful things he did to her—to "awaken her dead soul."

One night I went to Crowley's studio, on the northeast corner of Washington Square. This time it was Lea who called "Come in" when I tapped on the door.

She was lying like a queen or princess of the Arabian Nights on a great low divan covered with cloth-of-gold—dressed in a robe of purple silk, ensconced amid luxurious pillows, her little white feet encased in slippers of scarlet vaire.

Crowley, who paid not the slightest heed to my entrance, was squatting, cross-legged on the hard floor, with folded arms, like a Thibetan Llama or some old Asiatic god. He was intoning to Lea, with closed eyes, a part of the love canticle from one of his own mystical rituals. His voice, low and vibrant, came as from a man speaking in a dream.

"—but to love is better than all things.

"If under the night stars of the desert thou presently burnest mine incense before me, invoking me with a pure heart, and the serpent flame therein, thou shalt come to my bosom.

"For one kiss wilt thou then be willing to give all; but whoso gives one particle of dust shall lose all in that hour.

"But always in the love of me and so ye shall come to my joy.

"Pale or purple, veiled or voluptuous, I who am all pleasure and purple, and drunkenness of the innermost sense, desire you.

"Put on the wings, and arouse the coiled splendor within you—" More of this—in a silence unbroken save for the rise and fall of the mystic's voice—and I went away feeling as if I had intruded in a temple.

But do not get the idea that I am going to paint Aleister Crowley on these pages as a saint. I am not moralizing. I am writing these things neither as a defence nor as a denunciation. I am trying to depict the man as he is—giving you the good and bad with equal frankness—and I want to tell you that by any standard of morality you yourself may choose to apply, you will find as you read on that he was the most amazing mixture of good and bad that has ever existed in human form. I shall tell you things about him that will force your admiration—and I shall tell you things that will strike you, if you are normal, with recoiling repugnance.

As you were reading just now of Crowley's mystical adoration of Lea—of Lea lapped in luxury and worshipped as a queen—you may have thought, "Well, after all, what romantic girl might not be intrigued and pleased by such wooing?"

But wait. Another afternoon, within a week, I returned to Crowley's studio. This time the door was locked. But he let me in. In the center of the room was an enormous easel, so heavy and massive that it was almost a scaffold. And bound to this easel, facing it, was Lea—fastened by the wrists and ankles, her arms outstretched like a woman crucified, her dress stripped from her shoulders, her white flesh criss-crossed with red stripes.

Seeing my amazement, Crowley greeted me with a diabolical grin and tossed a broken dogwhip into the corner. "I have been awakening the Dead Soul," he explained cheerfully. "She doesn't object. If you are troubled with chivalrous scruples you can ask her. She wouldn't thank you if you tried to interfere. Permit me to explain that the efficacy of pain as a spiritual stimulus is a subject misunderstood and neglected by the modern woman. Sit down."

From Lea, all this time, not a word, not a sob, not a plaint. "She is engaged in holy meditation," Crowley continued. "Our conversation will not disturb her."

And while Lea stood there, still bound, like a picture of some unwritten martyr, Crowley calmly made me a learned discourse, which I wish I could reproduce, of the importance of asceticism and whipping and fasting and voluntary torture and mortification of the flesh as practiced by holy men and women and early church fathers of the middle ages.

If I convey the idea that Crowley, at this period of his extraordinary career in America, was occupying himself solely with the domination of one woman, I am giving you a wrong picture of his character. The man's dynamic energy was terrific. He was writing from five to seven thousand words per day on the manuscript of the *Equinox* volume which was later to involve A.W. Ryerson, the Detroit publisher, his wife and half a dozen other beautiful Western women in the "O.T.O." scandal, which has not yet reached its end; he was beginning to paint the pictures which later caused an unforgettable sensation and another scandal still later when they were exhibited at the Liberal Club; he was conducting mystical séances which were arousing the serious interest of some of America's leading physic authorities; and he was bringing under his influence, in one way or another, many women, some of whom were destined later to figure in his strange career.

The most interesting of these was Kitty Reilly, a tall New York girl, whom Arnold Genthe, a judge of beauty, regarded as one of the most extraordinary types he had ever seen—a girl of about twenty-two, with an enormous mass of flaming red hair, sea-green eyes, and a disdainfully curved mouth that suggested the women of the Burne-Jones and Rossetti paintings.

She was in love with Leon Kennedy, a Dutch artist, whose fantastic paintings are well known among modernists in Paris and New York. Kennedy was also a mystic, but of a totally different type from Crowley. Crowley believed that supreme spiritual exaltation could be obtained by either extreme of living—that is, through drugs, orgies, excesses and debaucheries—or by fastings, mutilations and mortification of the flesh. Kennedy on the other hand, believed there was only one "way"—complete subjugation of the physical senses and living by the spirit alone. Consequently he wanted Kitty Reilly, who was engaged to him, to consent to a marriage which would be a "spiritual union" only. He admired Crowley as a "great mystic," but deplored his "wickedness."

Kitty and Kennedy both frequented Crowley's studio to listen to his brilliant talk. No drama would ever have come of their association if Kennedy hadn't suddenly become interested in "psychochromes" (soul-paintings). He had delved deep into occultism and believed that he had won the ability of seeing people's "auras," the mysterious, luminous, colored emanations which are said to radiate visibly from every human being like the piebald aereoles of the saints in sacred art. Science, by-the-way, is inclined to believe in these emanations but doubts that they can be detected by any human being. Kennedy, however, thought he could see them plainly as the nose on your face. And so, he set about doing the portrait of Kitty's soul—the result with curves and swirls photographically reproduced on this page.[1] Unfortunately the colors cannot be reproduced, for it is the colors that were most important. According to the mystics, blue stands for spirituality, yellow for intellectuality, purple for perfection, and red for passion.

---

1 The image in question has not been reproduced here, due to, amongst other things, copyright restrictions.

Aleister Crowley watched the progress of this painting with sardonic interest, and commented on it with a biting wit—insisting that Kennedy was painting a picture not of Kitty, but of a creature that existed only in his own one-sided imagination.

About this time, with the picture two-thirds completed, Kitty and Kennedy, with a crowd of half a dozen other people, were in Crowley's studio one night, listening to him talk. It was impersonal conversation on the history of Egyptian religion—the kind of stuff you would expect to hear from some professor of archaeology, but Crowley managed to make it human and fascinating.

Kitty, along with the rest, became absorbed and interested. Her eyes were glued on Crowley's face. Suddenly Kennedy interrupted to cry out:

"My God, her aura is turning red!"

"It's always red, you fool!" retorted Crowley.

Kennedy buried his face in his hands. Kitty, a little heartless toward her fiancé, and perhaps a little tired of his "spiritual adoration," beamed on Crowley, and seemed pleased at having suddenly become the center of interest.

Crowley, who was a master of the unexpected, whatever else you may say of him, turned to Kennedy.

"My son, you have always regarded me as a wicked man. Now I, Baphomet, The Beast, am going to give you some good advice. And it will be precisely the advice you would get from your old-fashioned Methodist family preacher in Georgia—that is, if you happened to be in Georgia and to be a Methodist.

"Kitty loves you. It is true that in loving you she loves a simpleton, but that is her affair. Also you love her. She is a woman and you are a man. Your talk of 'purely spiritual unions' is silly rot. Keep it up and you'll lose her. Besides, it's human. Here is my advice: Take Kitty to the nearest church and marry her—unless she prefers a home wedding. Go on a long honeymoon with her—to Holland. Kitty will make a magnificent mother. After you have had a child or two—then do all the soul-paintings of her you want. Paint her in blues and greens and all the colors of the rainbow. Paint her as a purple cow, if it pleases you. But make her happy first."

Kennedy answered:

"A. C., I think, for once, that you mean well, but you do not understand. Kitty is a pure spiritual soul—see, now! Her aura is already becoming blue again—"

"You're hopeless!" cried Crowley. "But, no! If common sense is no good, I'll try another way! You, with your crazy colors! Pale blue, is she? Well, in spite of you, I'll do you the favor of turning her red for you—permanently—with the Mark of the Beast!"

And before anyone had divined his intent, Crowley leaped at Kitty and sank his teeth in her neck! It was quicker than the leap and bite of a dog or wolf—and over more suddenly. I don't think he touched her at all with his hands. Crowley was back in his chair, grinning like a devil. Kitty, after one sharp scream—of rage as much as pain—was holding her handkerchief to her throat.

"My God, this is terrible!" cried Kennedy, busy helping Kitty staunch the slight flow of blood, but not making the slightest attempt to retaliate against the man who had bitten her.

Kitty, not really badly injured, was denouncing Crowley in the most violent language a well-bred girl could think of. Beast and swine and mad dog were some of the epithets she hurled at him. It required no "mystic" to see that Kitty's aura was "red" at that moment. She was as angry as only a red-haired woman can get.

Crowley, not a whit disturbed and evidently hugely enjoying the scene he had made, still grinned as he replied:

"My dear, you are ungrateful. It was all for your good, I assure you. The act required great self-sacrifice on my part. I do not care for human flesh as a diet."

The climax of this amazing drama over the "spiritual aura" of Kitty Reilly (after all, it was but a minor scene in the bigger melodrama of Crowley's activities in America) came one night in my own apartment, which was then at No. 23 Christopher Street.

Kitty and Kennedy had dropped in. She was watching us at a game of chess. The doorbell rang. It was Crowley.

"Do what thou wilt shall be the whole of the law," he said with pompous solemnity, and added, with a grin at Kennedy, "but that implies you must have brains enough to know what you really wish."

"I shall do what I want—and it's this," replied Kennedy, trembling with rage. "I want you to let Kitty alone. If you ever so much as touch her or speak to her again I'll break every bone in your body."

Crowley sat down, Kennedy, white with anger, made a pretense of going on with the chess game. Crowley was smoking a cigarette. He made it glow red and, quick as a cat, jammed it inside Kennedy's collar, saying, "All you need is stirring up."

Kennedy clawed at his neck until he had ripped open the collar, and then leaped like a wild animal on Crowley. They were about equally matched and rolled over and over the floor, pounding and choking each other. Over went my center-table, down crashed a mirror, and the struggle ended, with my interference, in a deadlock.

They went apparently still hating each other. But they were a strange crew. And you'll be surprised at the sequel. Kennedy finally took Crowley's advice—and thanked him for it. Kennedy and Kitty were happily married—a real marriage. They went to Holland, and just the other day I had a picture postcard from them, sending "kindest regard to everybody."

In the next chapter I shall go more seriously into the "black magic" which Crowley practiced here.

CHAPTER III.

THROUGH the tangled and obscure details of the Ryerson divorce scandal in Detroit, which is just now being aired in the Michigan courts, the name of Aleister Crowley is sparking from day to day—with little scraps of evidence, like lurid lightning flashes, that promise amazing revelations—only to plunge the whole affair into deeper blackness and mystery than before.

It is developing that Albert W. Ryerson, rich publisher and owner of a big office building and a magnificent home, grew interested in Crowley's cults, publishing one of the volumes of Crowley's *Equinox*, and became a member, according to his friends, of the "O.T.O." which has many secret lodges in America and Europe.

Ryerson's first wife, Vida Marsh Ryerson, filed a divorce suit against him on the ground that he was practicing the "Do what thou wilt" code of morality said to include "free love."

Then, according to the court evidence, Ryerson found himself a second wife, Bertha Bruce Ryerson, a "bobbed-haired, fiery beauty," who was "to become the priestess of the cult," and who admitted on the witness stand that she was known to the initiates as "Bruce of the O.T.O." Ryerson became enraged at her, and they separated when he discovered the extent to which she had fallen under the influence of Crowley's philosophies.

And now, today, a third wife, Mazie Mitchell Ryerson, is denouncing Ryerson and seeking to divorce him, on the charge that he was practicing Crowley's wicked rites and sought to convert her to them.

Other prominent Detroit people have become involved. Other divorce suits, it is said, are pending. I shall tell more of this amazing tangle later—and a strange story it is, surpassing the most extraordinary plot ever read in fiction.

But now I want to expose and reveal the deeper and bigger mystery that lies behind it—"the mystery behind the mystery," which has only been hinted at in the court proceedings now going on—the true nature of the secret cult which started the Detroit scandal and the strange rites and ceremonials which have been used by Aleister Crowley to gain the mysterious world-wide power and influence he wields as supreme head of the modern "Devil-Worshippers."

I have told you that when I came to this phase of Crowley's unbelievable character I would produce the evidence of reputable and well-known witnesses to substantiate the extraordinary facts. One of these witnesses was in New York recently—Harry Kemp, poet and novelist—who has actually attended and seen with his own eyes one of the Satanist ceremonials, the nature of which has only been hinted at in a veiled way in the Detroit evidence.

Harry Kemp is on record as saying, "What I tell is so incredible that I shall be laughed at and called a liar—by those who do not know. But I wish to call attention to the fact that I give the name and address of Aleister Crowley, and that I am willing to make affidavit that everything I say is true.

"Crowley himself invited me to witness this ceremonial.

"In answer to my knock, the door was opened by a girl in a straight black robe. Entering, I found myself in a large, high-ceilinged studio, the atmosphere of which was colored a deep blue with the reek of peculiar-smelling incense. The place was divided with high-hung black curtains into three separate rooms.

"In the first room stood row on row of books bound in black and marked on their backs with queer, distorted crosses wrought in silver. The second room was fitted up with divans and liberally carpeted with multitudes of cushions tossed here and yon. In the third and larger room stood a tall, perpendicular canopy, under which the high priest (Crowley) sat during the cele-bration of the 'Black Mass.'

"Directly in front of it, on a floor tessel-lated in mosaics with parti-colored patterns and marked with cabalistic signs, stood the 'altar,' a black pedestal, to the top of which was affixed a golden circle. Across the latter lay a golden serpent, as if arrested in the act of crawling.

"I heard someone behind a curtain play-ing a weird, Chinese-like air on some sort of stringed instrument. The 'feel' of the whole place was decidedly uncanny.

"After the high priest of the Satanists had himself shown me about, we withdrew to the library, which was then inspected.

"In it seemed to be gathered all the mad books of the world—rituals of obscure sects, huge tomes on magic, white and black—and all the mystics were there—Bachman, Paracelsus, Swedenborg included.

"We sat before the fire, the high priest and I. He talked of magic and mysticism—and he knew what he was talking about.

"Then I saw the 'Black Mass.' I had arrived before the appointed time and was now shown to a seat near one of the black curtains and well in the background.

"One by one the worshippers entered. They were mostly women of the aristocratic type. Their delicate fingers, adorned with costly rigs; their rustling silks, the indefinable elegance of their carriage attested to their station in life.

"Everybody wore a black domino with a hook which concealed the upper part of the face, making identification impossible.

"Hung with black velvet curtains, the place had a decidedly sepulchral aspect. There was a fitful light, furnished by a single candlestick having seven branches.

"Suddenly the flame went out and the place was filled with subterranean noises like the sound of a violent wind moving innumerable leaves. Then came the slow, monotonous chant of the high priest:

"'There is no Good; Evil itself is Good. Blessed be the Principle of Evil! All Hail, Prince of the World, to whom even God himself has given dominion!'

"A sound as of bleating filled the pauses of these blasphemous utterances. Gradually the darkness lightened to a gray gloom—the very ghost of light—and moving shapes became distinguishable.

"I could hardly believe my eyes as I observed what followed.

"Amid floating clouds of nauseating incense a great crystal sphere rose slowly from the floor, and from it ascended a shape like a white puff of cloud. It wafted off, alighting on the floor, and assumed the form of a diminutive nude black being. Another cloud rose from the globe, and yet another, to materialize in the same manner. These were supposed to be the incarnations of evil spirits. They bleated and capered about in absolute nudity, weaving a grotesque dance in the gloom to the music of a hidden drum and flute.

"At this juncture a woman cried to be taken out and went into hysterics. Tearing off her mask, she revealed the fair face of a girl of the pure-blooded type of Anglo-Saxon beauty. She was quickly led away, and the rites were scarcely interrupted, so intent were the worshippers on their observances.

"They began to moan and sway. The candles became lit again of their own volition. Aleister Crowley, in the role of the high priest, stepped forward to the altar, from which he took a short, curiously shaped knife. He tore open his robe at the chest. His eyes were bloodshot and stony and fixed in their sockets, as if the man had gone into a trance. His chanting grew more and more frenzied. He began gashing his breast with the knife, and now he grew calmer. His disciples came forward one by one, and he made a mystic mark in blood on each of their foreheads as they knelt.

"After this the affair rapidly degenerated into an indescribable orgy. Men and women danced about leaping and swaying to the whining of infernal and discordant music. They sang obscene words set to hymn tunes and gibbered unintelligible jargon. Women tore their bodices, some partially disrobed and one fair worshipper, snatching the high priest's dagger from a small table, slashed herself across the chest. At this all seemed to grow madder than ever. I repeat, I could scarcely believe my eyes. All modern civilization, all the moral ideas taught for centuries, were thrown to the winds. All I desired was to escape unobserved."

I quote Harry Kemp because his sworn corroboration will help you to believe the even more startling revelations I have to make about this hidden sect, which even now—at the very moment you are reading this—still has its worshippers and its secret "temples" scattered through many cities in America.

More startling? Yes! Because Harry Kemp did not see the real "Black Mass"— the amazing, prescribed and uniform secret ritual which is the central "key" ceremonial of the Devil-Worshippers the world over— and which, until now, has never been accurately described in a newspaper. Various accounts have appeared in print from time to time purporting to describe the ritual of the unholy ceremony, but they fall far short of the truth.

I have seen the real "Black Mass." I know what I am writing about—for I have also studied its origins. And the "Black Mass" is an actual ceremonial, as devoutly believed in by its participants as any form of devotion. In the early Middle Ages a strange sect called the Manicheans branched off from an orthodox Christian church. They believed that Satan was the equal of God—that God and Satan were two separate, equal beings, who ruled together over the universe, and that both had to be propitiated. They spoke of God and Satan as two equals, making wagers, taunting each other, and discussing the fate of poor human beings, just as two equal hereditary kings, for a moment friendly, would discuss their antagonistic interests. Therefore, the Manicheans argued that in order to be on the safe side it was best to worship both. And so they did. They were denounced, of course, as heretics, but the strange cult has survived—in the modern Devil-Worshippers.

In order to perform a real "Black Mass" three things are absolutely necessary.

A renegade priest who has actually been ordained in the church.

A maiden "pure in mind and heart and body."

A consecrated wafer.

Aleister Crowley believed that he was a priest, because he believed that he was a reincarnation of Eliphas Levi, the Abbe

Constant, an able scholar of the church, who made an elaborate study of magic.

The girl was selected from the "high priestesses."

Imagine a large studio, hung with black curtains to represent a chapel. Dim lights. The "worshippers," men and women in black hoods, are seated as solemnly and quietly, on benches, as if they were in a real church. Their attitude is devout. Presently they kneel.

The "altar," on an elevated platform at the end of the room, is hidden by a thick veil. Slow music, of a distinctly religious tone, is wafted from muted violins.

The "priest" enters slowly from a side door. He is garbed precisely like those you have seen, except that the cross on his surplice has given place to a different symbol. He is followed by the "high priestess," who serves as his acolyte. She is barefooted, bareheaded, with her hair hanging down over her shoulders, garbed only in a robe of scarlet. She swings a censer, in which incense is burning, while the "priest" bows before the veiled "altar." Then the "priest" begins to recite a Latin ritual, the form of which, it is said, has been handed down secretly for hundreds of years. The word

"Lucifer" is substituted for "God" and the word "Evil" is substituted for "Good."

The worshippers kneel at the beginning of the invocation, and the curtains of the "altar" are drawn aside to an accompaniment of tinkling bells and swinging censers.

In the background of the "altar" and at either side are flickering candles in seven-branched candelabra and single candlesticks. Immediately behind the "altar" proper is a distorted silver cross.

The "altar" itself is a wooden block about four feet high and three feet across the top, covered with black velvet.

Lying upon this "altar" is the girl nude.

Her head thrown backward at right angles to the body, her arms and streaming blonde hair hang perpendicularly along the right side of the block; and her lower limbs, bent at right angles at the knees, hang down the left side—in such a way that her whole body makes a sort of cover for the "altar," forming the top and two sides of a rectangle.

She lies motionless as a statue, absolutely white in the dim light, like a figure cut out of marble.

On her chest is a broad-based golden chalice or cup containing the wine—unholy travesty.

The girl herself is delicately formed, of slender sculptural outline—apparently about nineteen or twenty years of age. Except for her slight breathing I can imagine she is made of wax or stone. I do not know who she is. Her features are only dimly discernible, but I do not think that I have ever seen her before—or that I shall ever see her afterward.

As if in a trance, she continues to lie motionless for a half hour, while the "priest" intones his profane ritual, the violins still playing their muted, religious music, the "worshippers" joining in the litanies and responses.

But the litany is a prayer to Satan to "redeem us from virtue."

At the culmination of the "Black Mass" the "priest" lifts the cup from the living "altar," drinks of the wine, and sprinkles a little of it on the girl's body, where it gleams like tiny drops of blood on the white skin.

The girl lies motionless on the "altar," untouched by the "priest," throughout the ceremonial. The curtains are drawn and the abominable performance is ended.

This is the real "Black Mass." No "magic." No orgies. No saturnalias. Unholy, blasphemous, but quiet and solemn.

The orgy which Harry Kemp witnessed, and at which I was not present, was a different sort of ceremonial. The only part of his evidence which I have found difficult to reconcile with the facts—in the light of my long and intimate knowledge of Crowley and his priestess—is his description of the actual materialization of the dancing figures of evil spirits that came out of the smoke.

I have seen Crowley try to do that—and fail. Perhaps he didn't expect to succeed. One never knew when the real mystic ended and the charlatan began. He sincerely believed that he was able to invoke demons and spirits and actually to talk with them and make them do his bidding—but he declared to me that he had never been able to see or touch them—to make them physically visible. I asked him outright about the materializations which Harry Kemp described, and Crowley admitted to me that they were illusions—partly explained by the hypnosis of the spectators and partly by tricks which Crowley had learned during his long stay in India.

But that Crowley had, and has today, powers of some kind which he is able to command and use—however rationally you may choose to explain them—is a fact admitted both by his followers and his enemies.

In the next chapter I shall tell how the influence of Aleister Crowley began to spread in America; how he suddenly began to paint weird and amazing "spirit-inspired" pictures; how he was hailed by his disciples as a "second Gauguin"; how the big exhibit of these paintings at the Liberal Club in New York broke up in a dreadful riot, and how the pictures were torn from the walls when it was discovered that they all had a "terribly wicked, hidden meaning."

CHAPTER IV.

"I hear you're doing a series of articles on Aleister Crowley," said Captain Achmed Abdullah in the card room of the Lafayette.

There were several of us at the table, having coffee—an Englishman, an Irish Poet, a French art critic and two Americans.

I assented.

The Oriental tale-writer exploded. "Again that scoundrel—that cousin of pigs!"

"But I say!" interrupted the Englishman. "He's by way of being a wonderful poet, you know, and he's written a very remarkable novel."

"Just the same," cut in one of the Americans, "I think Abdullah's right—a torturer of women, after all, that fellow Crowley, and a thoroughly wicked man."

"How very curious," said the other American, who is a professor at Columbia. "I knew him only as a quiet and able scholar—a brilliant authority on religious history."

Then it was the Frenchman's turn. "Aleister Crowley?" he said. "That's the man whose work I saw on exhibit in Paris last Spring. I didn't know he wrote at all. I thought he only painted—the weirdest and most astonishing pictures you ever saw."

Aleister Crowley, the painter! That, too, was one of the sides of this amazing, many-sided character—and with the Frenchman's words a crowd of recollections came—of how Crowley first began painting in America, without ever having touched a brush before in his life—and of the wild scandal and riot his pictures caused when they were put on exhibition at the Liberal Club in New York.

It was an astonishing episode, as you shall see.

By that time Crowley had lived for some months in America and his work as a writer and mystic was beginning to be known. Lea, "The Dead Soul," was reigning with him as a sort of "queen and slave" in a bigger studio, magnificently appointed, into which they had moved, at 63 Washington Square

South, with enormous windows overlooking the beautiful square and showing a long vista of lower Fifth Avenue. She was a cultured woman and a charming hostess and they entertained a great deal—many distinguished people—in a more or less conventional way.

But Crowley was working, enormously hard, sometimes from midnight steadily to noon of the next day, writing the new volume of his *Equinox*, which was destined later to start the big Ryerson scandal in Detroit.

One day Crowley came home with a great hamper filled with blank canvasses stretched on frames, his pockets full of tubes of paint, and carrying in his hands an array of brushes that would have been amply sufficient for Raphael and Titian combined.

"My familiar spirit visited me in the night," he explained, "and commanded me to paint. I have been under the misapprehension that I was a great poet. Clearly, I was mistaken. Paint is my real medium. I am destined to become one of the outstanding artists of my age."

Whereupon, with the utmost solemnity, and with an industry that would have won praise from the professional optimists, he began to paint.

And, mind you, he knew nothing whatever about it. He didn't know how to mix the paints. He lacked the most rudimentary training in drawing. And he disdained to learn in any ordinary way. He was afraid it would "cramp his originality."

He painted, at first, like a child, or an industrious baboon, which had by accident acquired oils and brushed—and which was working like an automaton.

I still have some of those first canvasses. I have kept them as a curiosity. They are the most awful smears you can imagine. The figures, arms, legs, torsos, faces are all "out of drawing" and the primary colors laid on with an inconceivable crudity and glare.

After some weeks of this, he said to me one day, "I began to be discouraged. I think my familiar spirits, my daemons, have something important to express through this new medium—but they don't know a thing about technique—they don't even know the mechanics of painting. It's very unfair to me. And, if you don't mind, I think we had better run up to the Metropolitan Museum and take a look at Rembrandt's 'old woman.'"

So we climbed atop a Fifth Avenue bus and presently stood in front of the greatest art treasure in America—and one of the greatest oil paintings in the world.

Crowley looked at it for a long time. He walked back to the opposite wall and studied the picture from a distance. He got so close that his nose pressed against the glass. He cursed the glass because it didn't permit him to touch the painting with his fingers. He considered the possibility of visiting the museum at night and stealing it. And he came away silent.

After this visit he began "mixing" his paints, a thing it hadn't occurred to him to do before, and to practice line drawing with crayons and charcoal.

And then, gradually, he began to paint the amazing pictures that have come to be the despair of art critics here and abroad. Some of them are grotesques which surpass in horror the worst nightmare you have ever dreamed. Others have a touch of primitive beauty that suggests the earliest Chinese paintings. They are "all wrong" by any academic standards, yet they are unique, and when you see them you can't forget them. "He can't paint at all," said one critic. "He's the worst painter who ever lived." Another declared, "Art is in a transitional stage. This man is crude. But who knows? It may be the crudity of a genius."

Leaders of the ultra-modernist school in America began to be greatly interested, though they didn't entirely approve. Crowley's notoriety was beginning to spread, and with it whispers of "devil-worship," black magic, love cults and hasheesh orgies. Naturally, people were a little afraid of anything he did.

An effort was made to stage an exhibit in a big Fifth avenue gallery. It failed. "This fellow is dangerous and disreputable," it was said. The Liberal Club, that stronghold of the real, first Greenwich Village "intellectuals," was approached. The members were interested, but afraid of Crowley's reputation.

It was at this moment, it so chanced, that Frank Crowninshield, a magazine editor, wrote and published an article about Crowley that put him in a different light. If Crowninshield, an established authority, a man of power and standing and taste, said that Aleister Crowley was "important," that settled it. He was.

The Liberal Club read Crowninshield's article with hungry interest. According to this tribute, Crowley was "one of the most extraordinary of our British guests—a poet, explorer, mountain climber, an adept in esoteric philosophy—in short, a person of so many sides and interests that it is no wonder a legend had been built up around his name in his own lifetime.

"He has published more volumes of poetry than he has lived years," the writer continued, "and has climbed more mountains than he has lived months. The *Equinox*, his work on occultism, is only a part of the gigantic literary structure which he has built up in the past five years; yet the work contains the stupendous number of two and a half million words.

"In 1900 he explored Mexico without guides. Two years later he spent many months in China. In 1906 he crossed China on foot. The success of his drama, *The Rites of Eleusis*, in London in 1910, did not tempt him to settle there for long, as he was next heard of in the heart of the Sahara.

"As a naked yogi he has sat for days under the Indian sun, begging his rice. Like every true magician, he has experimented with hundreds of strange poisons, in order to discover the Elixir of Life. He has devoted much time to the art of materializing divine influences, and of rituals inherited from the Gnostics and Rosicrucians. He shocked the orthodox by his book, *The Sword of Song*—which was virtually an attack on everything established—but soon compelled them to forgive him because of the religious fervor of his next volume—a book of devotional hymns.

"He has hitherto lived in Paris when not on his travels. One of his friends is Augustus John, the painter, who has done some wonderful sketches of him."

The Liberal Club was impressed. "So," said its members, "this Crowley is evidently a great man. Poe and Baudelaire and a lot of other great men were not what they should have been morally, but what's that got to do with art? Let us, by all means, exhibit Crowley's pictures."

You would have imagined that Crowley, who had the simple vanity of a child, would have been pleased with Crowninshield's article. Not at all. "Alas," said he sadly, "this man has entirely mistaken me; my only claim to distinction is as a painter!" And I honestly believe that at that moment he believed it.

So Crowley's paintings were hung on the walls of the main salon of the Liberal Club, and cards were sent out announcing the exhibit. All Greenwich Village came afoot and the uptowners came in their limousines.

An astounding array of pictures it was—witches, goblins, giants, devils, grotesques, "holy men," misshapen nymphs dancing in such landscapes as never before were seen on land or sea—but the staid and soberest members of the Liberal Club looked in vain for anything "wicked" or "immoral."

The truth was, that any young girl could have looked at all of Crowley's pictures without seeing a thing to shock her moral sense. A child could have looked at them. It might have been frightened, but it wouldn't have seen anything "naughty."

Why, then, you are wondering, did the affair end in a raging scandal and the stripping of the pictures from the walls?

It was a surprising climax, not without its element of savage, Rabelaisian humor. The affair hasn't yet died down. Only a day or so ago I was able to get from a member of the club some of the memorandum records, which I shall presently quote. It was generally understood that Crowley's paintings were "symbolic." Near highbrows and dilettante old ladies, adjusting their monocles and lorgnettes, gazed in astonishment at the canvasses. Finding ordinary adjectives inadequate, they would end by exclaiming knowingly, "Oh, how symbolic!" But what they were symbolic of no one ventured to suggest, for nobody knew.

One afternoon Crowley himself was there, vastly delighted with the sensation he was creating—all tricked out in a lemon-colored waistcoat with agate buttons, English knickers, tasseled brogues, and a shaven head that made him look, aside from his clothes, like a Buddhist priest or a Bayswater convict—whichever you pleased.

A group had gathered around one of his canvasses which bore the seemingly innocent title of *May Morn*. It was like many of his pictures, a sort of nightmare in vivid colors.

Crowley's *May Morn* abounded in the most violent of contrasts. Look at it today, if you can locate the canvas, and study its peculiarities. The weird painting shows a background of bleak, Chinese mountain landscape. In the foreground looms a dead tree, and hanging from it by the neck is the body of a witch or hag. From behind the tree a bearded face, whimsically like that of Bernard Shaw, peers out. It might be the face of a devil, or of a philosopher. In the back distance, by a stream, a man is playing on a flute, and a golden-haired, half-clad girl is dancing in joyous abandon. In the foreground are enormous misshapen mushrooms and toadstools.

Several persons were discussing it aloud and puzzling over the painting's incongruous title. "Dear Mr. Crowley, won't you please explain to us, in your own words, the meaning of this picture?" asked a kindly old lady of the group, who was "so interested," she said, "in all modern movements."

"Certainly, madam," responded Crowley in his most suave and punctilious English manner. "The subject is very simple. The artist represents the dawn of the fay, following a witches' celebration, like that described in the Brocken scene of *Faust*. The witch is hanged, as she deserves, and the satyr looks out from behind a tree. In the background all is beautiful Spring and the nymph dances joyfully to the piping of the shepherd."

"How very charming," beamed the old lady, "and so delightfully simple, now that you have explained it. How can anyone say that your pictures are immoral?"

But it wasn't so "delightfully simple" as the old lady thought. The next afternoon one of the governors of the club visited the exhibit, I am told, in a state of violent excitement.

"This man, Aleister Crowley," he began, "is a monster, a blasphemer, an abomination. He is trying to destroy everything that is sacred and holy—and these pictures of his, apparently innocent, are in reality, the hideous, veiled propaganda of his wicked cult. You heard the glib, lying explanation he gave of the picture called *May Morn*. Now listen to the real interpretation of that picture, written by this man himself, for his equally depraved initiates."

And, unfolding a paper which he had taken from his pocket, he read:

"This picture is symbolic of the New Aeon. From the blasted stump of dogma, the poison oak of Original Sin, is hanged the hag with dyed and bloody hair, Christianity. The satyr, a portrait of Brother D. D. S., one of the teachers of the Master Therion, represents the Soul of the New Aeon, whose word is, 'Do What Thou Wilt.'

"The shepherd and the nymph in the background represent the spontaneous outburst of the music of sound and motion, caused by the release of the Children of the New Aeon."

The storm that followed is still talked about by Liberal Club members. A violent discussion immediately broke out. Some of the more vehement participants were for burning the pictures or calling in the police. But others took the stand that if the pictures were worth looking at they should be allowed to remain.

The first faction prevailed, but not unanimously, and amid a storm of violent disputing, which nearly led to physical violence, the pictures were stripped from the walls, and word was rushed to Crowley to have them taken off the premises immediately.

In the next chapter I shall tell how I became acquainted in New York with the beautiful violinist, Leila Waddell, who had been the "high priestess" of Crowley's "O.T.O." cult in England, and how I learned more of its mystic séances and practices, including a revelation of the astounding alleged "crucifixions" which were participated in by members of the "sect."

CHAPTER V.

PRETTY MAZIE RYERSON, once an artist's model, who charges her elderly husband, Albert W. Ryerson, rich Detroit publisher, with trying to convert her to the mysterious "O.T.O." cult, of which Aleister Crowley is the world head, made extraordinary accusations that Ryerson subjected her to physical "tortures" as part of this "conversion."

How many other women there are throughout the United States, throughout the world, under the influence of this strange cult—some of them may be reading these very lines—who could tell even more amazing stories if they were willing to speak!

I am thinking at this moment of Leila Waddell, the beautiful violinist and noted concert artist, who was Crowley's "high priestess" when he was at the height of his fame in

England, openly holding elaborate "mystical rites," attended by many notables, in the big town house he occupied at that time—and of the strange circumstances of the talented Leila Waddell in New York.

"What's that got to do with Mazie Ryerson's revelations in Detroit?" you may be wondering.

"And what connection has it with the alleged 'mystical crucifixions' which you promised last week to tell us about in this chapter?"

That, too, shall be explained.

In the *Equinox*, one volume of which Ryerson had published as part of the "Bible" of the "O.T.O.," there are many references to mystical "crucifixions" as part of the experiences of initiates and adepts in the cult. One of the extraordinary entries begins:

"Fra P. was crucified by Fra D. D. S., and on that cross made to repeat this oath," etc. There is an illustration entitled *The Crucifixion of Fra P.*

To what extent these "crucifixions," as described in the book, were literal, physical experiences—if at all—and to what extent they were purely symbolic rituals, I am unable to specify. But before I go further with this account, it is necessary to give you, briefly, some additional light on the character of the strange figure behind it all.

Crowley, whatever else he may be, believes he is a true mystic—perhaps one of the greatest mystics living. Some of his poetry, embalmed in the anthologies, may suffice to give him, after he is dead, at least a minor rank among the immortals. And the various cruelties which I have described—the branding of Lea on the chest and other incidents—are part and parcel of this side of his character. Throughout my extended and intimate acquaintanceship with him, which has lasted several years, I have never known him to hurt a woman—or any living creature—for the sake of sheer wantonness or amusement. He was not a Caligula or a Nero. In fact, it enraged him, as it does most upper-class Englishmen—and decent people everywhere, for that matter—to see or hear of needless pain inflicted on any helpless being whether human or animal.

"How can this be?" you ask. "A man who, by your own account, whipped a frail girl?"

Well, unfortunately for consistency, this is not a fictional story in which the "villain" can be made altogether a villain, nor is it written to prove or disprove anything—to "defend" Crowley, or to denounce him. It is written to paint him as he is, good and bad together, one of the most amazing figures of modern life.

Crowley spent years in the Orient, studying occultism in a land where to become "holy" one must lie on spikes and cut himself with knives, or sit so long in one position that the muscles become atrophied. Crowley "derives" also (though he might violently deny it) from those curious mystics and saints of the middle ages who engaged in similar practices. In some of the modern treatises of William James, late great Harvard psychologist, and in old books of lives of the saints, you can read of many such characters—the Spanish nun who achieved sanctity and ecstasy by having herself beaten with whips to which had been fastened jagged leaden pellets; the early French bishop, who wore beneath his gorgeous vestments a chain around his waist that continually cut into his flesh; or ole Saint Simeon Stylites, who lived for many years on top of a bare pillar, exposed to the blazing sun, storms, winds and snows.

And Crowley, today, in the twentieth century, like these old "holy men" and "holy women" of another age, is seeking, as an incidental part of his complicated doctrines, to revive this curious method of "sending the soul into the infinite" to explore deeper mysteries of life.

These practices, too, are curiously interwoven with his "Black Magic"—and this brings me directly to the "mystical crucifixions."

One day, in his New York studio, I asked Crowley to tell me something of this alleged practice. He had a great deal to say about symbolism in mysticism and magic, and gave me a hair-raising account of the "Black Mass" used by sorcerers to work harm to their enemies. In the course of a ceremony dedicated to Satan, a toad is crucified upside down, and by the recitation of certain charms the enemy is supposed to sicken and die as the toad expires.

"But I can tell you something much more interesting," he added, "the story of a girl whom you may some day meet. But perhaps I'd better read you an account of her as I have set it down in writing to be included in the *Equinox*."

And he read from a manuscript (he afterward gave me a copy, which I have before me now), the recital which you shall hear.

Before quoting him I must give you the "key" that will explain the significance of what he tells, for it is so fantastic that, without a "key," the normal mind might see in it only a meaningless melodrama of insane horror. After you have read it and heard the sequel you may still think it is merely such a melodrama—but it contains a deeper element.

You may have read in your school books, in the poetry of Tennyson and in tales of the days of chivalry how people used to believe in "love philtres," charms, amulets, talismans, by which, through magic, they were able to obtain the love of persons indifferent to them.

The story Crowley told me was of a modern girl who secretly believed and engaged in "magical" practices, and who had a talisman which she tried to make use of in this way. With a self-sacrificing girl cousin, who was her submissive victim, she went to dreadful lengths, Crowley's narrative related; to restore to this talisman the potency which she believed it had lost.

Here is the essential part of the manuscript from which Crowley read—written, as you will note, with a sort of "literary flavor."

"Patricia Fleming ran up the steps into the great house, her thin lips white with rage. For the third time she had failed to bring the man she wanted to her feet. She looked into her riding hat. There in the lining was the talisman she had tested—and it had tricked her.

"'What do I need?' she thought. 'Must it be blood?'

"She ran, tense and angry, through the house. The servants noticed it. 'The mistress has been crossed,' they thought. 'She will go to the chapel and get ease.'

"True, to the chapel she went, locked the door, lit a lantern, dived behind the altar, struck a secret panel, and came suddenly into a hiding hole, a room large enough to hold a score of men if need be.

"At the end of the room was a scarlet post, and tied to it, her wrists swollen by the whip-lashes that bound her, was a girl, big boned, strong and partially unclad.

"'What, Margaret! So blue?' exclaimed Patricia. "'I am cold,' said the girl in a low voice.

"'Nonsense, dear!' answered Patricia, rapidly divesting herself of her riding coat. 'There is no hint of frost. But you shall be warm yet, for all of that.'

"This time the girl writhed and moaned a little.

"Patricia took the faithless talisman from her hat, which she replaced on her head. The talisman was a piece of vellum, written upon in black. She took a hairpin, pierced the talisman, and drove the pin into the girl's shoulder.

"'They must have blood,' she said. 'Now, see how I will turn the blue to red! Come, don't wince dear.'

"Then with her riding whip she struck young Margaret between the shoulders.

"A shriek rang out. She struck again and again. Great weals of purple stood on the girl's back; froth tinged with blood came from her mouth, for she had bitten her lips and tongue in agony. Then the skin burst. Raw flesh oozed blood that dribbled down Margaret's back. Still Patricia struck and struck in the silence, until the tiny rivulets met and waxed great and the blood touched the talisman. She threw the bloody whip into a corner and went down on her knees. She kissed her cousin, she kissed the talisman, and again kissed the girl.

"She took the talisman and hid it in her clothing. Last of all, she loosened the cords, and Margaret sank in a heap on the floor. Patricia threw furs over her and rolled her up in them; brought wine and poured it down her throat. She smiled kindly, sadly, like a sister.

"'Sleep now a while, dear,' she whispered, and kissed her forehead——

I broke the silence that followed. "Do you mean to tell me seriously," I asked Crowley, "that things like that have survived the middle ages—that there are people who really believe in such practices—that such things are actually done by anybody in this modern twentieth century?"

"Next week," said Crowley, with an enigmatic smile, "if you care to meet her, I'll introduce you to a girl who looks like 'Patricia.' She's coming to America. Wait a minute; I'll show you her picture."

From a little iron-bound trunk which contained pictures and clippings about himself and the doings of his cult, saved from old magazines and newspapers, he produced a portrait of Leila Waddell, the beautiful violinist. From the details of the picture and from the text underneath, I judged that Miss Waddell had been a "priestess" of the "O.T.O." cult while it was at its zenith in England—at the time when Isadora Duncan, the dancer; Augustus John, the painter, and Aimee Gouraud were attracted to the ceremonial rites in Crowley's London house—attracted, no doubt, by their artistic beauty without knowing anything of the hidden mysteries behind them.

Miss Waddell, in the photo-engraving, was shown clad in a mystical robe, bare-footed, seated upon a throne, wearing upon her head and chest the insignia of the "O.T.O." The picture was from *The Sketch*, one of London's leading magazines dealing with society and art. The caption read:

"In a modern ceremony to invoke Artemis (a Pagan goddess) this is the lady of mystery, the violin player. On another page of this issue will be found an article dealing with 'A New Religion.' Apropos of this illustration of the lady who played the violin at Mr. Crowley's at-home, at which an experiment was made in the effects of a ceremony to invoke Artemis, we may quote the following lines from the article: 'After a long pause, the figure enthroned took a violin and played, played with passion and feeling, like a master. We were thrilled to our very bones. Once again the figure took the violin and played an evening song, so beautifully, so gracefully and with such intense feeling that in very deed most of us experienced that ecstasy which Crowley so earnestly seeks.' The lady in question, it may be added, is Miss Leila Waddell, who is very well known as a concert artist in England, Australia and New Zealand."

Other photographs of Miss Waddell, I discovered afterward, appeared in several of the volumes of Crowley's mystical books—always in the garb and role of a "priestess" of the cult.

I noticed the dedication on the manuscript from which Crowley had just been reading the amazing story. It contained the initials "L. W."

A week later, true to his promise, he took me to meet Miss Waddell, who had arrived in America—in fact, to have tea with her. It was in a hotel just off Fifth Avenue, in her own apartment. She proved to be a lovely, cultured woman, a charming hostess and a brilliant musician, for I later heard her play exquisitely.

We talked of many things, but I didn't quite dare to bring up directly in my conversation with her such a subject as magic. It seemed utterly impossible that two such cultured, well-bred, thoroughly modern and cosmopolitan English persons, as she and Crowley were at that moment, could have anything in common with the strange beings of whom I had glimpses—and more than glimpses—during my acquaintance with Crowley and his books.

Behind it all there is such a mass of facts which will never be known, of mysteries that lead into the secret places of China and the Orient, into old and forgotten cults on the one hand, and into events which, on the other, are taking place today in American and English cities, that I doubt if the whole truth will ever be known of Crowley and his strange associates.

Poor little Mazie Ryerson, artists' model, out in Detroit, complaining that her husband tried to "torture" her in connection with the "O.T.O." I wonder how much she knows of the intricate labyrinth behind it all—the astounding background and broader drama of which her broken happiness was only a tiny part, in spite of the big scandal it made in the Middle West.

In a like maze of bewilderment is the English girl, Betty May Loveday, who recently returned to London from Crowley's "abbey" at Cefalu, with amazing charges against the man the *London Daily Express* calls "The Beast 666" and "The Purple Priest." Betty May Loveday's husband died at Cefalu; her charges against Crowley are blood-chilling. But this, and Crowley's answer to them, I must reserve for a later chapter.

In the next chapter I shall take up a side of Crowley's character and of his activities in America which I have hitherto left untouched—his experiments with hasheesh and other Oriental drugs, which he himself used for a time and introduced to his "disciples"—and what came of it.

CHAPTER VI.

EVERY week in the magazines and newspapers, you see new exposés of the extraordinary spread of the drug evil in America.

You have probably read of the brave fight, which ended in his death, that Wallace Reid made, after drugs had gripped him: of Evelyn Nesbit, who fought unsuccessfully her battle against cocaine and heroin and escaped their awful thrall, only to be brought down with pneumonia that almost snuffed out her life: of thousands of other people, less well known, whose bodies and souls have been destroyed, or who have recovered only after suffering terrible tortures.

You have read, and are still reading, from day to day, of the enormous extent of the narcotic traffic, of hundreds of thousands of dollars' worth seized in this or that city.

Usually these narcotics of which you read are morphine, cocaine, heroin, opium, veronal. Occasionally, but rarely, you come upon a paragraph or a passing mention of hasheesh—that strange Oriental drug which figures so extensively in the magical tales of the East.

That you hear less of hasheesh than of the other narcotics is not because it is less dangerous or less harmful, but simply because it is less known to America and the Western World.

Indeed, it was so little known as a narcotic in the United States that it was left completely out of the list in the passage of the Harrison Federal anti-narcotic laws, and up to two years ago you could buy it (though practically nobody did) in any well-stocked drug store. It is a vegetable product, the essence taken from the flowering tops of Indian hemp.

It stood on the shelves labeled simply, "Cannabis Indica—Poison," and usually the druggist himself only knew of it as an ingredient in the manufacture of certain corn plasters and occasionally in veterinary medicines.

He little dreamed that his "Cannabis Indica" was simply a distilled solution of hasheesh—the dangerous Oriental drug of the "Arabian Nights" stories.

There is sometimes a danger, when giving the public "inside information" such as I am presenting in this chapter, that it will serve, instead of a warning, merely as a "lead" by which drug addicts can get a new source of supply. But there is no such danger in this case. The door has been shut. New laws have been passed. And the authorities have learned enough, at least, about hasheesh to make it as inaccessible as any other banned narcotic. Furthermore, anyone who would experiment with this poison, after first learning the whole truth about, as it will be told in these pages, would be crazy.

I learned what I know about hasheesh—and I know a good deal—from Aleister Crowley, that strange mixture of genius, debauchee, and mystic, who has touched at one time or another, I believe, every height and depth of which humanity is capable.

I was present at a number of the so-called "hasheesh orgies" which went on in Crowley's New York studio, at 63 Washington Square South, and I propose to give you an accurate account of one of them.

The little that is publicly known about hasheesh outside the Orient is a mixture of truth and fable. As Crowley himself said, few Europeans or Americans "have dared to crush in arms of steel this creation of the Djinn; to steal form its poisonous scarlet lips the kisses of death—only to read in its infinite sea-green eyes the awful price of surrender—black madness."

The words sound extravagant, high-flown, but they are not. Crowley himself was one of the first persons, and one of the few Englishmen, who ever experimented extensively with this dangerous drug. He learned about it first in the Orient, where many yogis and "holy men" employ hasheesh to help them attain the mystic state of "Samadhi," or "oneness with the universe." He took it to "loose the girders of the soul," just as these Oriental mystics did. He escaped from the "black madness," but you must remember that he is a man of extraordinary, almost superhuman, will-power, who had engaged in many other practices that would destroy the body and mind of the average person, and has managed to come through them, scarred, but vigorous.

From his experiences he has analyzed the effects on the brain of hasheesh—a scientific analysis that has been accepted as authoritative.

The first symptom, psychologically, is that you are thrown into an absolute state of introspection. You perceive your thoughts, and nothing but your thoughts. Your will is not at first involved. It is a state of powerful looking-inward of a purely impersonal kind.

But with a larger dose the images of thought begin to pass more rapidly through your brain. And they are no longer recognized as mere thoughts, but imagined as actual, material things. They become visions and hallucinations. The ego and will become alarmed and may be attacked and overwhelmed. Being swept away on the tide of restless and uncontrollable visions is a terrible experience.

You may get glimpses of ineffable beauty and splendor, dazzling, intense, passionless bliss. But there come, too, the awful shapes of delirium and madness, destroying the mind that fails to control and dominate them. The despair and terror of the universe become concentrated in yourself. What poignant agony, what moaning abjectness! What vain folly to seek paradise in drugs!

I know these things now. I did not know them when Crowley invited me to take hasheesh in his studio with a party of his friends. I accepted because of the extraordinary accounts I had read in Baudelaire, Poe, Dumas and certain Oriental stories of the effects of this mysterious drug.

Three other persons had been invited: Natasia Fedorovna, a beautiful Russian actress, who had come over from Paris; Ai Nasaki, a Japanese poet, who did extraordinary sword-dances; and an Englishman, who had lived for years in the Orient as a member of the diplomatic service. Of course, Lea "The Dead Soul," was also present. So there were six of us, four men and two women. We had been asked to eat lightly and to bring pajamas and dressing gowns. Hasheesh, like opium, sometimes produces nausea if one has eaten heavily. Anything but loose clothing would be uncomfortable, as hasheesh, Crowley said, should be taken lying down.

The big studio had been arranged for the occasion. Three mattresses, covered with heavy Oriental tapestries and piled with cushions, had been laid on the floor alongside the low couch.

Crowley, clad in heavy Chinese pajamas of dark blue, was seated at a little table, preparing the drug, which he had in a bottle, a nauseous, sticky, dark-green liquid solution, with a characteristic sickening odor something like that of decaying grass.

Twelve drops of it constituted a dose, to be repeated every hour or so if effects were slow in coming. Some of it he put into ordinary druggist's capsules, and some he dropped into small glasses of sherry, to take away the bad taste. You could either swallow the stuff in the sherry, or take it like a pill in the capsules and wash it down with a glass of wine or coffee.

A half hour, an hour, sometimes an even greater length of time, elapses before you begin to feel any effects. So after each had taken the prescribed dose we made ourselves as comfortable as possible on the couch and cushions to await what would happen.

Nasaki, the Japanese, who had promised to dance, did not take any hasheesh at first. He went into an adjoining room and presently came out in the dress of an old Samurai warrior, but without the hideous mask that sometimes goes with that costume. In broken English he explained that he was going to do the dance of a battle in a mountain pass which a handful of Japanese had held against invaders until all but he was killed, and the latter left wounded and dying on the field. He did it to the accompaniment of an odd chanting, a rhythmic recitation in his native tongue. It was pantomime rather than our American idea of dancing. But it was very effective. Retiring and stripping himself of everything but a cloth around his loins, he did another dance called "The Bat and the Willow Tree." It was clear and more precise than the so-called "Greek classical dancing," but very beautiful. He told us it had been danced in exactly that manner in Japan since the seventh century, handed down from generation to generation, and that not a single gesture had been changed.

"We should begin to feel something soon," said Crowley, who was lying on the hard floor, staring at the ceiling. We were all more or less silent and presently Crowley began to chant, in a low, deep monotone:

"Oom ma na padma oom; oom ma na padma oom."

You have probably seen the syllables before, perhaps in Kipling's account of the Red Llama, *Kim*. It is the chant, or "mantra," used by the Buddhist holy men to work themselves into a trance state. Over and over again, always in the same change-less, deep monotone, Crowley repeated the supposedly magical words. As if from a great distance one heard the repeated, booming, "Padma oom!" like some great faraway, muffled, brass band. And presently it subsided. Perhaps he had gone into the trance he sought, I thought.

As for the rest of us, we began to be, frankly, a little bored. There we lay, in the dimly lighted, quiet room—and nothing whatever happened.

"Do you feel anything yet?" the Englishman asked the Russian girl.

"No, monsieur," she responded in French "—unless a slight tingling in my toes, but I think that's just because my foot's gone to sleep." And so we talked, intermittently, rather stupidly, it seemed to me, for some time.

Suddenly, without warning, the drug "got" me. A great surge like an electric wave seemed to run through my blood and nerves and to sweep me into another world. My last normal thought was one of alarm and a feeling that I had "let myself in" for a good deal more than I had expected. This wave passed as quickly as it had come, and left me, I imagined, with an amazing clarity of thought, such as I had never experienced in normal moments. The conversation was still going on. Instead of seeming stupid now, it was astounding and brilliant. In every trivial word spoken by others I discovered, or imagined that I was discovering, a wealth of hidden and important meanings. I joined in the conversation, and then my first actual hallucination occurred. I was talking to the Russian girl, who lay about four feet from me. I could see her face, and her white forehead gleaming in the dim light. As she spoke, her words seemed to be coming from her brain instead of from her mouth—and I saw them, as plainly as I now see the lines on a sheet of paper. They were a fan-shaped network of tiny golden shafts of light, like incandescent wires, that shot out from her forehead toward mine. My own thoughts, likewise, became golden wires or rays that darted from my forehead to meet hers. In the sentences or thoughts where we understood or agreed, the rays from her brain seemed halfway to meet mine and merge into a single ray, establishing a connection between her brain and mine. When we disagreed, or didn't fully understand what the other was saying, the rays or wires became tangled.

But this was nothing to what happened next. Suddenly, as I lay quiet, staring, the ceiling of the room began to shoot up, the walls seemed to recede, and I was in an enormous, well-like hall, in which I was as small as an ant looking at the sky. The voices of the others came to me as if from an immense distance in space. A little while ago, there had been an empty open fireplace, near where I lay. This fireplace now was the arched doorway of a cathedral, its top higher than the tallest mountain, lost in clouds.

My mind, racing madly, and completely beyond control, was seizing on every impression that came to my senses from outside, and distorting it. Lea, "The Dead Soul," rose to get a drink of water. I watched her passing across the room. It seemed to take her hours, days, and weeks—eternity. She was like a person seen walking across the desert—seen from an immense distance, so that she seemed going at a snail's pace. It would take her centuries, I thought, and I forgot all about her. Presently she must have turned on the water, for I heard the sound, but again distorted it, and imagined myself to be in the Garden of Versailles, surrounded by flowers, palaces, statues, while the great fountain was playing, sending its jets and cascades against the blue sky.

But don't imagine that all my hallucinations were pleasant. They soon turned from beauty to nightmare and horror. Natasia, the Russia girl, must have been getting a totally different effect from the hasheesh. Where it had seized my mind and sent it off into fantastic imaginings, I think it must have taken hold more directly on her emotions, her nerves, her physical self. For I saw that she had stripped off most of her clothing and was dancing alone, as if totally unconscious of the others' presence, in a mad abandon, as if every nerve and muscle of her body had been galvanized by a series of electric shocks from which she could not escape.

At first this seemed very beautiful, but suddenly a horrible thing occurred. Her rounded flesh, as she danced, seemed to be melting away, and then where I had seen a beautiful woman, I saw a hideous thing form the tomb, a million times more frightful than any skeleton, doing an awful dance of death. I wanted to cry out—to shriek, but my throat was dry and contracted. It was this that suddenly turned my hallucinations inward—made me acutely conscious of my own body. And this is one of the characteristic "hells," I am told, in which the confirmed hasheesh fiend inevitably suffers unspeakable tortures. I became aware of mysterious movements going on within me, all horribly distorted and magnified. My heart was an enormous hammer, beating with tremendous force, as if each stroke would burst through my chest. My breathing, really normal, I learned afterward, was like some mighty wind sweeping in and out of my lungs. There was a fearful dryness in my throat. I thought I was going to die. This, too, passed, and there came other visions—some beautiful—some so hideous that they cannot be described. Finally I went to sleep, in a deep stupor, that lasted until the next day.

Mind you, this was just an "experiment" with hasheesh—an experiment which I tried because I wanted to "know,"—which I repeated once, at the expiration of more than a year—and which I have never repeated again.

If anything I have said has given you the slightest inclination to try such a crazy experiment, I want to tell you briefly the experience of an American who began it as an "intellectual test" and ended by becoming an addict. He finally was saved, after going through unspeakable tortures, but I want you to remember that there are others who began the same way and ended in suicide or madness. This particular man, made a record of one night of horror through which he went. From this record I shall quote. He had awakened, while under hasheesh, in the middle of the night:

"It was an awakening which, for torture, had no parallel in all the stupendous domain of nightmare sleep. Beside my couch stood a bier form whose corners drooped the folds of a heavy pall; outstretched upon it in state lay a most fearful corpse, whose livid face was distorted with the pangs of assassination. The traces of a great agony were frozen into fixity in the tense position of every muscle, and the dead man's finger nails pierced his palms.

"Two candles at the head and two at the feet of the bier made the ghastliness more unearthly. I pressed my hands against my eyeballs till they ached, in a vain effort to shut out the sight.

"But, oh, the unspeakable horror! I behold the walls of the room slowly gliding together, the ceiling coming down, the floor ascending, as of old the lonely captive saw them, whose cell was doomed to be his coffin. Nearer and nearer I am forced toward the corpse.

"I cowered in abject fear. I tried to cry out, but speech was paralyzed. The walls came closer and closer together. Presently my hand lay on the dead man's clammy forehead. I made my arm as straight and rigid as a bar of iron, to resist, but of what avail? Slowly my elbow bent with the ponderous pressure, nearer grew the ceiling. I was forced into the embrace of the corpse. I stifled. I was insane with terror. The stony dead eyes stared up into my own—a maddening peal of laughter rang close beside my ear. I was being crushed in those horrible arms—and I felt all sense blotted out in the darkness."

As for Aleister Crowley, if what I am writing were fiction instead of truth, I might point my moral by telling you that he had become an addict, a "hasheesh fiend"—but it would be a lie. That extraordinary man, one in a million, whose admirers say he is protected from everything because of his "holiness" and whose enemies think he has the power of the Devil incarnate, plunged into these excesses when it pleased him.

Less than a month after the experience of which I have told you, he was camping on Aesopus Island, up on the Hudson, hard and brown as an athlete, painting "Do What Thou Wilt" in enormous red letters over the sides of the rocks, for passengers on river steamers to see. How he "went broke" in his "hermitage" on Aesopus Island, and how he sent to New York and asked a young countess to come to the island, I shall tell in the next chapter.

CHAPTER VII.

I just got a radio message from Aleister Crowley's "holy abbey," perched on a Sicilian mountainside above Palermo, Sicily, overlooking the Mediterranean.

It was a "commercial wireless" and it came "collect," full rate. It was in answer to a cable I had sent asking him to mail me certain photographs.

Two or three words would have sufficed for his answer.

Instead of that, when I tore open the envelope, this is what stared me in the face: "DO WHAT THOU WILT SHALL BE THE WHOLE OF THE LAW. EVERY MAN AND WOMAN IS A STAR."

And after three lines of this, at about ten dollars a line, three words tacked on the end like an afterthought, "am sending pictures."

I suppose I should have been surprised and annoyed, but I wasn't. Crowley has never let his own money—or that of his friends—interfere with preaching his extraordinary "new religion."

I happen to know that, on quitting Cambridge University, he had a fortune that ran close to a hundred thousand pounds. So far as I know, he hasn't got a nickel of it left—and most of it has been spent (squandered, if you like) preaching, teaching, writing this "Do What Thou Wilt" doctrine.

If you happen to take a trip up the Hudson this Spring, in one of the boats plying between New York, West Point and Albany, you will pass a rocky island in the river, some hundred miles above Manhattan.

It is called Aesopus Island. And if you look closely at the flat rock surface fronting the channel you may see traced upon it, in huge, crimson, weather-beaten letters:

"Do What Thou Wilt Shall Be the Whole of the Law."

This sign must have amazed thousands of tourists when it was bright, new and easily legible. I wonder if any of them ever dared to put it into practice.

Of course it was Crowley who painted it there. I can see him now, in the basement of the Brevoort Hotel, with his baggy English knickers, solemnly announcing to a surprised circle of Greenwich Villagers that he was going into a "magical retirement." I can see him—and their increasingly surprised faces—when he later exhibited the equipment for his "magical retirement"— an old canoe, two moth-eaten blankets and five immense cans of red house paint.

No provisions. Not even so much as a box of soda crackers. And not a cent in his pocket. He had spent his last twenty-five dollars on the paint.

"But how are you going to eat?" someone asked him.

"Remember Elijah and the ravens," he replied with a superb gesture. "Heaven will provide!"

Blasphemy? Or a childish faith? I haven't the remotest idea. But it actually turned out that Providence, or luck, or something, did provide.

It didn't send Crowley manna, but something much more modern, and infinitely better suited to his whim—a pretty Italian countess in riding breeches, who not only supplied food for him in his "magical retirement," but cooked for him and waited on him like an Oriental slave.

However, that is getting ahead of my story. You shall have it all presently—both sides of it—Crowley's own version and that of the pretty little countess. And a rare story it is. You would have to go back to Chaucer to find its parallel. Sir Gilbert Frazer, of Oxford, who writes about comparative religions in the Encyclopedia Britannica, once said about Crowley that his chief fault was that he had been born "five hundred years too late—or five hundred centuries too early."

Where did he get it, the "Do What Thou Wilt" doctrine, which he has been preaching so recklessly and passionately all his life, and will preach, I think, until he dies?

I happen to know, and there are a great many people, I believe, who will be interested to learn the real truth about it, briefly. Crowley's family belonged to a sect of religious bigots in England, called the "Plymouth Brethren." There is nothing quite like it now in the United States. It corresponds approximately to the worst of the narrow-minded "Puritan" type that flourished in New England in pre-Colonial days—the kind of false Christianity that takes all the joy out of life and believes that happiness is wicked. His childhood, therefore, was dismal and repressed. This distorted, so-called "Christianity," that was not real Christianity at all, came to him simply as a series of "Thou shalt nots," forbidding him to do everything he wanted to do—including many of the most harmless pleasures. When he began to think for himself he rebelled violently against it, and came to the conclusion that any religion which manifested itself in such a way was wrong—was an obstacle to human happiness and freedom.

Yet he was by nature strongly religious—like all mystics. So he set about to find a new religion. If he had begun amid different surroundings, if Christianity had come to him in a faire guise, I think it quite likely he might have become a Christian mystic. As it was, he shook the dust of England from his feet and buried himself in Central Asia in the hope of finding something better. He spent years in the study of religions, found none made-to-order that pleased him perfectly—and so he invented one for himself. Because the Commandments of Christianity, which he hated, seemed a series of "Thou shalt nots," he took as the sole commandment and creed of his new religion, "Do What Thou Wilt Shall Be the Whole of the Law."

It is really based, at the bottom, on an extraordinary faith in human nature. He believes that by becoming absolutely "free" in thought and deed, a race of supermen and superwomen will finally be evolved. Indulgence in the grosser appetites he regards as "unimportant." The weak, who succumb, he thinks, should be eliminated anyway, and so will be no loss to humanity. The strong, eventually, will rise above most passions—and by a curious twist he thinks they will "rise" quickly be experiencing them. A dangerous doctrine, obviously, for poor weak mortals to learn that our own Emerson preached a variation of it. So did Thoreau. So did Swinburne. So did Shelley. So did Walt Whitman. But they contented themselves with merely "preaching" it, as a sort of philosophical abstract for intellectuals only. The difference in Crowley's case is that he actually practices it, and when he preaches it—he shouts it to the crowds.

So it was that Crowley, starting up the Hudson on a fine Summer morning for his "magical retirement" on Aesopus Island, carried with him five gallons of red house-paint, instead of the food that would have been taken by a sensible man.

Part of the Aesopus Island is farm land, and consequently the farmers of the neighborhood came out to it frequently. Crowley landed there at night, and when some men arrived the next morning to tend to their unripened crops they beheld him, by the water's edge, in front of a shabby little tent, kneeling on an Oriental rug, garbed in a monk's coarse, black robe, praying to the sun.

Courteously and with the utmost solemnity he explained to them that he was a "holy man," retiring for a time from the world to pray for the salvation of humanity. He explained further that his "holy views" had prevented him from bringing along any food, and that he would be very much obliged if they would occasionally give him something to eat.

Inside the shabby tent they caught glimpses of richly bound books. Here, at any rate, was no ordinary beggar. You would expect that a hard-headed up-State farmer would have scant patience with such a peculiar visitor. But Crowley had a way of getting along with all sorts of people when he wanted to. And for a couple of weeks the farmers actually did feed him.

It was like a chapter from the life of some long forgotten hermit who lived in the

Middle Ages. Nobody but Crowley would ever have thought of doing such a thing in twentieth-century America on the Hudson River. The farmers brought him eggs, jugs of milk and early "roasting ears." And Crowley, squatting all day on his prayer-rug in the sunshine reading his mystical books, getting what he needed to eat without having to raise his hand, was blissfully happy.

It was during these early days of his "magical retirement" that he chalked out "Do What Thou Wilt Shall Be the Whole of the Law" in enormous letters on the rocky cliffs facing the river and filled in the outlines with his red paint, so that all the excursionists on the river boats could read the inscription. The neighbors let this pass as a crazy whim though they didn't like it.

However, it was a totally different thing that got Crowley "in dutch" with the natives. Like many another general whose campaign was going well, he made a grave tactical blunder. He put on a pair of knickers, and with them a pair of Scotch plaid golf stockings, with tassels on the cuffs.

Now for some curious reason, "up-State" farmers have an intense dislike of knickers. They may forgive a man for being a forger or a thief, if there are extenuating circumstances, but a man who will deliberately wear "short pants" arouses immediately their distrust and dislike. Crowley, the "holy man" in a coarse black robe, was one thing; but Crowley garbed like a "dude tourist" from the city, with tassels on his golf stockings, was a different matter. So they brought him no more food. They pointed out bluntly that if he wanted it he could go to the nearby "general store" and buy it, like any other "camper."

For the next two days Crowley fasted. But this was carrying holiness a bit too far. So the "prophet" pulled up his belt another notch, got to the mainland, hiked to the nearest small town that had a telegraph station, and sent a rush message "collect" to the pretty little Countess Guerini, who was then in Westchester County, inviting her immediately to visit his "Summer camp" on the Hudson, and giving her explicit instructions how to get there.

The Countess Guerini had known Crowley when he was rich, in London. She had also encountered him when he was hunting big game in Africa. "Summer camp" sounded elaborate and attractive. And taking for granted she would find servants, bungalows, motor-launches, cool drinks and cooler breezes, she came.

Garbed in nifty riding breeches, with a big trunk full of sports clothes and semi-formal evening gowns, she got the shock of her life. She arrived at twilight and was dumped, with her trunk, on the rocky shore of Aesopus Island by a boat that immediately put back to the shore. There was Crowley, kneeling on his prayer-rug, back in his monk's black robe. And there was the shabby little tent. And there stood the petite and exquisite Countess in her sports clothes.

"I am at my devotions," said Crowley solemnly. "You must wait." While the Countess waited for a half hour, with growing anger and suspicion, the "prophet" addressed esoteric prayers in Hindustani to the rising moon.

"And now that this disgraceful farce is over," said the angry little Countess, "will you be kind enough to conduct me to your Summer camp?"

"But, my dear, where are your eyes?" demanded Crowley with a diabolical grin and a pompous wave of his hand. "You have arrived. The camp is here. And I hope you've brought something for supper."

La Guerini gazed with horror at the shabby little tent and with increasing rage at Crowley. "What a dirty trick! I shall go straight back to the city tonight."

"You can't do that, my dear; you can't get off the island. You'll have to spend the night. You needn't be afraid. You may have this palatial pavilion for yourself. I shall sleep, or meditate, among the rocks."

"But I must have my bath!" she rejoined.

With another of his wicked grins Crowley spread out his arms as if to embrace the whole Hudson River. "But I'm afraid you'll have to supply your own soap and towels," was his remark.

This was too much—much too much—for the Countess. She burst into hysterical tears and fled into the despised tent, which offered the only refuge, and sobbed herself to sleep, determined to leave at dawn.

Why didn't she leave the next morning? I really don't know. But she remained. And she was not in love with Crowley, then or at any other time. She was a good soul beneath her frills, and from what I know of women I think she stayed because she discovered that Crowley was hungry—that he hadn't had anything to eat for three days.

In the mass of contradictions that made up Crowley's character, there was a streak of something that, for lack of better words, I might describe as pathetic, childlike. It was the thing that made many people, men and women, keep a sincere affection for him, despite his dreadful faults.

Every little while the "Monster" and "Beast" became just a sort of bad little boy, posing and doing naughty things to shock the grown-ups—and then you felt sorry for him, and liked him, and forgave him everything.

I think it was this side of his character, more than anything else, that kept the Countess on Aesopus Island. For she stayed there nearly two weeks—and people who saw them beheld a situation that you would regard as fantastic and impossible even in the plot of a musical comedy.

The very next day she went over to the mainland in a rowboat, visited the "general store," and came back with a lot of canned stuff and other food.

And Crowley—with a selfishness that was also characteristic—now that his stomach was full again and food provided for tomorrow, paid not the slightest attention to the young woman who was making this sacrifice.

Once assured that she was not going to desert him, he went back to the business of his "magical retirement" as if she were no more than a human servant—or a slave of the lamp sent by magic to wait upon him.

All day long, squatting or kneeling in his coarse black robe, he would pray or meditate. Half the night, with the aid of a flickering candle, shielded by a crevice in the rock, he would read his mystical books.

The Countess, still in her rising breeches—which were about the only garments that she had brought fit to be worn in such a place—cooked for him and waited on him as uncomplainingly as if she had been captured in the Arabian desert or bought in the slave-market of Samarkand.

"It was the first time I had ever done any work," she said afterward in New York; "the first time I had ever done anything to help anybody else, and I believe I really liked it."

And so this extraordinary episode ended without scandal. But presently Crowley returned from his "magical retirement" and took his "Do What Thou Wilt" doctrines to Detroit, where they helped break up homes, got onto the front pages of the newspapers and ended in the Ryerson scandal, about which I shall tell in my next chapter.

CHAPTER VIII.

"I still bear the whip-marks, welts and bruises of my twenty-nine-day horror as the trial bride of Albert W. Ryerson, the O.T.O. leader in Detroit."

That's the way a "love cult," as interpreted in the Middle West, appealed to one beautiful American girl, who says she would rather be dead than go through it again.

She is Mazie Mitchell Ryerson, third wife of the rich Detroit publisher, who put on the market Aleister Crowley's volume of the mystical *Equinox*, and from whom she fled at the end of her "trial marriage."

She went on record as declaring, when asked the reason for her renunciation of the "O.T.O.":

"There are thousands of members of such secret organizations in this country today. Girls cannot be too careful in protecting themselves against such men. Trial marriages are dangerous if they have anything to do with the O.T.O. I hope my terrible experience will be a warning to other girls."

Crowley went away before Mazie Ryerson appeared as the "persecuted heroine" of this extraordinary human drama. His direct participation ender after he had gone to Detroit, preached his "Do What Thou Wilt" doctrine to a little coterie of prominent persons, established a "temple" and published his book—with the help of Ryerson.

Crowley says Ryerson is a "weak fool," who totally misunderstood his doctrines.

Ryerson says Crowley is a "scoundrel," an "inhuman devil," and denies that he ever really became a member of Crowley's cult.

Be that as it may, this is what happened:

Crowley appeared in Detroit to establish a chapter of the "O.T.O." He was a guest in Ryerson's home and Ryerson published his book. Then twice during the year the "O.T.O." loomed up in Detroit court proceedings when shocked wives appealed for divorce because their husbands had become affiliated with this order.

There was a great scandal. The big book publishing house of which Ryerson was the head became involved, and Ryerson was charged with spending its money to further the "O.T.O."

Bertha Bruce Ryerson, a defiant, bobbed-haired and acrimonious beauty, who declared herself then the wife of Ryerson, was brought into court, where it was testified that she was to have become the "high priestess" of the new cult in Detroit.

Following that scandal, she and Ryerson separated. Crowley meanwhile had gone away. Later, Ryerson, middle-aged and rich, met and fell in love with Mazie Mitchell, a beautiful young art model. He said, at first, according to her story, that he wanted to adopt her as his daughter.

What then occurred, according to her version of the tragedy, she tells as follows:

"I was changed from an ignorant, innocent girl into a woman with knowledge of much that is evil, mysterious, horrible. I was initiated into the mysteries of the occult. I became acquainted with turbaned Hindus discussing theosophy, ancient cults, practicing magic and hypnotism.

"I learned for the first time that thousands of persons in the world today are practicing the secret rites of ancient cults and worshiping idols.

"I thought at first that Ryerson was just a kind, fatherly man, taking an interest in a young girl who was trying to earn her own living. What girl of seventeen would not feel flattered if a rich, middle-aged man wanted to make her his adopted daughter and heiress?"

She tells, then, how he took her to his luxurious apartments, hung with weird tapestries and gorgeously decorated in Oriental style. He treated her, at first, she says, exactly like a daughter, and promised to have adoption papers made out soon. But his two Hindu servants, Maneck and Jamsed, filled her from the first with un-easiness and fear.

Ryerson bought her an expensive mo-tor car, showered her with luxuries. But, according to Mazie Ryerson, the idea of adoption was very soon dropped.

"Well, Mazie," he said to her one night, according to her story, "the world may not think it quite the proper thing for you to be living here with me. It would be safer if you were my wife. If you are not certain you would like to be my wife, we can have a thirty-day trial marriage. At the end of that time, if you do not like me as a husband, you can get a divorce. I will not contest it."

He promised her, she says, jewels, clothes, a beautiful home, an artistic career. And she at last consented. They were married by a prominent rector of Detroit, and she was taken to Ryerson's magnificent estate on Riverside Drive, near Ford City, Ontario.

"I cannot describe the first three days and nights of my marriage. It is better for me and others to cast a veil over the terrible things that happened. If there had been any love in my heart for my elderly husband he would have killed it then. He subjected me to unspeakable tortures, both physical and mental."

What some of these ordeals were she describes, or hints at, later.

"It was on the third evening that he first whipped me. He whipped me until I was black and blue and almost fainting. I screamed and screamed, but it made no difference. He seemed to take a fiendish delight in my screams.

"When he released me I ran from the house. I didn't care where I was going. I hid under the porch, like a cowering, whipped dog, and lay there shivering all night. I determined to run away, to go back to my artist friends and make a living posing again as a model."

But even after this, Ryerson was able to persuade her to try life with him again, she says. He was good to her for a while.

Then, she says, he began to torture her again.

"He would awake me in the middle of the night and commence whipping me. Once he whipped me so hard and long that I lost consciousness. The marks are still on my body.

"One night he produced a book of clippings and told me of the O.T.O. Most of the stories were false, he said. I believe he certainly intended to make me a member of the cult. But he found me too determined to resist. I think that is why he commenced to beat me. He may have thought that by whipping and abusing me he could mold me to his will. But he couldn't.

"Soon after we were married strange people began to come to the house—mysterious, dark-skinned men from the Far East. Ryerson told me they were instructing him in old beliefs. Once there was a wild party and I was forced to be a member of it. I cannot describe it. I cannot tell you how much it revolted me.

"Sometimes when I threatened to leave him he promised to be good. At other times he said he would make it impossible for me to leave him and would 'fix it' so that I couldn't obtain a divorce.

"I became convinced that Ryerson was almost demented. he would talk to me for hours about reincarnation, telling me that he was King Solomon and I was Cleopatra. He boasted that he had a thousand wives scattered through the United States. All this bored me. I was just an average girl, not interested in this mystic stuff.

"I couldn't bear it any longer. Twenty-nine days after we were married I fled from Ryerson's beautiful home and went back to a life of hard work. I had no money, nothing I could turn into cash. But I would rather have died than live the life that an O.T.O. follower wanted me to lead.

"Ryerson has said that I eloped with his Hindu chauffeur. There is not a word of truth in that statement. We did leave the house the same day, but not together. When everybody was asleep, just before dawn, I slipped out, taking nothing Ryerson had bought me—just a few of my old dresses in a bag—ran to the street car and sought refuge with my friends in Detroit."

Ryerson paints another side of the picture, in which he "blames it all on the woman."

He denies he is an incarnation of King Solomon—but says his beautiful young art-model wife is a modern Cleopatra, Aspasia, Semiramis all rolled into one—"vixen" and "vampire."

He accuses her of being a bigamist and falling in love with his Hindu servant.

He says she was "heartless as a tigress and dangerous as a volcano."

He admits he "spanked her," but says it was for her own good, and implies that it "hurt him more than it did her."

Lest you doubt this, he explains that the "little tigress" turned on him and "sank her teeth into his arm."

And now he denounces her with fervor.

"It seems that I owe something to society and to the good of the girl herself," he says, "not to permit her to further conduct her career of destruction without a warning to the community as to the true character of this little vixen, who is a dangerous woman to be at large.

"Quiet, refined and demure, sweet, charming and young, she was experienced in wickedness, as I found out later, like a woman of forty. She boasts openly of being a vampire, one who can bring any man to her feet."

Although Ryerson published Crowley's *Equinox* and "O.T.O." ritual, and had Crowley in his home and was prominently present at the organization meeting of the cult at Detroit, he denies he ever participated in its ceremonies. It was not these doctrines, he says, that helped break up his home, but the hypnotic influence of an East Indian servant in the house, who went by the name of "Gim."

"Gim," he asserts, gained such an influence over the young wife that when the Indian was later dismissed she sold her jewels in order to supply him with money. This Mrs. Ryerson denies.

"One night when Mazie thought I was asleep," he says, "she slipped downstairs to the Hindu chauffeur's room. I followed quietly and heard her say that 'Daddy would raise the dickens if he saw me here.' He replied, 'He'd better not, because you know me. See this big knife! I can throw that thirty feet and land it in a man's heart. I could strangle him with a cord so cleverly that no one would know how he died. Then we could throw him into the river, pretend that he had been drowned, motor to Montreal, ship the car and go to India."

One of the most amazing charges Ryerson makes is that his wife was all the time secretly in the control of a bunch of Hindu "mystics" and criminals who used her for blackmailing purposes.

He said members of the gang threatened to cut his throat if he interfered between them and Mazie, and boasted they were going to "have a party which would last a year" after Mazie had "hooked" him for large sums of money.

After Mazie left him at the end of the twenty-nine-day marriage he says, "I had various propositions through taxi drivers and Hindus to deliver the girl over to me for sums ranging from $500 to $5,000. One of the propositions came from the Hindus through a lawyer. It was hinted that the Hindus had hypnotized the girl, and that she never would come back to me unless they could be persuaded, by my paying them money, to take off the spell.

"The Hindus have been active in their demands and getting bolder all the while. I have since learned that this gang is from Bombay, India, and is part of a bad organization there. They are posing in this country as healers and religious men—roles in which the gullible American public was only too willing to accept them, myself included. They fixed upon me as their prey, and after living upon my philanthropy for an entire Winter they broke up my home."

To say that these amazing events, coupled with other incipient scandals among the followers of the "O.T.O." in Detroit, have made a sensation in the Middle West, would be putting it mildly.

It is more than a sensation. It is an uproar. In the civil courts a suit was started by stockholders of the book-publishing concern, of which Ryerson was the head, to determine whether he was using their capital to help the "O.T.O." cult. In the divorce court there were sensational charges and counter-charges. The "Chalet d'Arts," the art school where Mazie Ryerson had posed as a model, was raided by the police, and large numbers of nude paintings and drawings were confiscated and destroyed.

In defending himself against the accusations brought by his pretty young wife, Ryerson added additional bitter counter-charges against her, in the course of which he said:

"I fell for her and am paying the price.

"When I tell my story I will let the public be my judge. I shall tell how she boasts of being a professional vamp; one who can bring any man to her feet; how she has vamped, she says, as her latest victim, a young newspaper reporter, whom she claims to have ensnared so as to get her publicity to enable her to get into the movies.

"I was also informed by a man, a fancy dancer, who claimed to have resided in India, how these fellows operated, and that the reporter was merely one of their unsuspecting tools. I shall tell how I was horrified to hear Mazie say that her gang was going to get Judge —— for sentencing a girl for eight years.

"She became defiant and bold because they claim that they have the newspapers and the police on their side. She would sing hymns before going out for the evening, place a Bible in my hand, telling me to be good, and inform me that she was going to the theatre with a girl friend, and in the middle of the night I would be called up and informed that she was in some cabaret.

"I had begged Mazie to allow this divorce to go through, sane and suppressed. She refused because she wanted the publicity. She finally did agree, and proposed that after she got the publicity for her to withdraw the suit if I would later give her a quiet divorce.

"I shall tell you how she pretended in her press story that she did not want alimony, yet in her suit claims it, listing my properties; how the gang seized upon the O.T.O. notoriety to use it for their evil, blackmailing schemes.

"Concerning the O.T.O., it can, so far as I am concerned, be dismissed briefly. A few years ago several prominent men met in an attorney's office in Detroit to be introduced to Aleister Crowley with a view of forming a chapter in Detroit, to organize a tentative lodge by acclamation without initiation or ritual, pending the arrival and approval of the rituals.

"I was one of those present at this meeting. A day or so later four of the men met with Crowley at the D.A.C. and organized a supreme grand council.

"The understanding was that both of the meetings aforementioned were merely tentative, pending the arrival and examination of the rituals, which were to be sent to the attorney for revision and approval. Some action would be put forth in initiations if approval was forthcoming. Mr. —— went to Salt Lake City to confer with a member there, and when he returned the rituals had arrived under seal for his eyes only. He advised dropping the matter, which was done.

"The newspapers of Detroit tried to make out that a love cult existed. The O.T.O. was not a love cult, nor did ever any exist in Detroit of which I was a member.

"A certain prominent attorney was elected its head at the D.A.C. meeting. When trouble came and unsavory notoriety I was made the 'goat' for the bunch, although entirely innocent, and I have, in my silence, practically laid down my life for my friends.

"My home has been completely ransacked at various intervals, my papers and books seized, my servants bribed, my library robbed, and I have been persecuted beyond endurance by people seeking evidence concerning the O.T.O."

In my next chapter I shall make public the complete text of the "secret, sealed ritual" delivered by Crowley "to ten prominent men in Detroit," and on which, it is declared by the Detroit police, the local "love cult," which resulted in these scandals, was based.

CHAPTER IX.

I recently received from Aleister Crowley himself—mailed from the "abbey," where he lives, surrounded by his "disciples," in Cefalu, Sicily—a copy of the secret ritual of the "O.T.O." cult, which he sent "in sealed envelopes," when he was in America, to "nine prominent men in Detroit," and which after his departure, precipitated the series of scandals culminating in the Ryerson divorce case.

It contains, as you will read, the formal creed of Crowley's "Do What Thou Wilt" cult.

It also contains a great deal of love symbolism, and a ceremonial in which the "high priestess," a beautiful woman, appears unclothed before the assembled worshippers and performs certain mystical rites.

This formula, for the "priestess," who divests herself of her robes, so amazing to the Anglo-Saxon sense of decorum, is really the center around which part of the Detroit scandal has raged.

It is charged by Crowley's enemies in Detroit, that he also communicated to a select "inner circle" of men and women, by word of mouth, the "unwritten ritual" of the "Black Mass," which is the carefully guarded secret ceremonial of the cult of Satanists or Devil-Worshippers.

The "Black Mass," which I mentioned in detail, in an earlier chapter, is a blasphemous ritual which travesties the Holy Communion. Its chief feature is that the "altar" on which the ceremony is performed holds the prostrate body of a nude girl—"a maiden pure in mind, heart and body."

While the "high priestess," who eventually divests herself of clothing during the ceremony, acts as a simple acolyte for the "priest," the girl lies motionless upon an altar-block, her head thrown backward, her arms and streaming hair hanging down one side of the altar, and her lower limbs, bent at the knees, down the other side. On her chest is placed a cup of wine, and at the culmination of the "Black Mass," the "priest" lifts the cup, drinks from it, and sprinkles some of its red drops upon the girl's figure.

It was common talk in Detroit that Bertha Ryerson, then wife of Albert W. Ryerson, rich book publisher, was to be the "high priestess" of the new cult. It is not recorded that Ryerson objected to this at first. But when the secret ritual became known, with a description of the garments which the "high priestess" should wear—and what, during a part of the ceremony, she should not wear—the "fireworks" began.

In the course of the wrangles which followed during which attempts were made by stockholders to oust Ryerson from control of his big book concern, he and Bertha Bruce Ryerson separated.

Afterward Ryerson married Mazie Mitchell, a former art model, who has also since separated from him. Strangely enough, she says she believes Ryerson's "cruelty" to her had as a secret motive a desire to force her to participate in the "O.T.O." practices, though he never demanded it outright.

Here is the ritual, which Crowley himself has supplied me, with permission to reproduce it for the first time publicly in America, and which I have had verified as being identical with the one circulated in Detroit:

The altar shall be seven feet long, three feet wide, and forty-four inches high. It shall be covered with a crimson cloth, embroidered with a sun-blaze. On each side shall be an obelisk or pillar. On the altar shall be an empty place for the Book of the Law, with six candles on each side. Below it is the "Holy Grail," or cup, with roses on each side of it, and on each side beyond the roses are two great candles. In front of the main altar is a small black altar. All this is enclosed within a great veil.

The officers of the ceremony are as follows:

The "priest," who bears the sacred lance, and is clothes at first in a plain white robe.

The "priestess," who must be a woman especially dedicated to the service of the "O.T.O." She is clothes in white, blue and gold. She bears the sword, suspended from a red girdle, and carries a wafer.

The "deacon," who is clothed in white and yellow, and who bears the Book of the Law.

Two children, who are clothed in white and black. One bears a pitcher of water and a cellar of salt: the other a censer of fire and a casket of perfume.

After the "deacon" has admitted the congregation, he places the book on the high altar, kisses it, turns to the worshippers and says:

"Do what thou wilt shall be the whole of the law. I proclaim the law of light, life, love and liberty."

The congregation replies:

"Love is the law, love under will."

The "deacon" and the people then repeat:

"I believe in one secret and ineffable Lord; and in one star of whose fire we are created, and to which we will return; and in one Father of Life, Mystery of Mystery, and His name is Chaos.

"And I believe in one Earth, the Mother of us all, and Her name is Babalon.

"And I believe in the Serpent and the Lion, and His name is Baphomet.

"And I believe in one Gnostic Church of Light, the word of whose law is Thelema.

"And forasmuch as meat and drink are transmuted in us daily into spiritual substance, I believe in the Miracle of the Mass."

Music is now played, and the children enter, followed by the "priestess," who places the wafer on the altar and adores it.

The "priest" enters, holding the lance erect against his breast, with both hands.

He gives the lance to the "priestess," kneels and worships it, and says:

"I am a man among men."

He takes the lance again and lowers it. He says:

"How shall I be worthy to administer the virtues of the brethren?"

The "priestess" replies:

"Be the priest pure of body and soul. Be the priest fervent of body and soul."

She robes the "priest" in scarlet and gold. He takes her by the right hand, and, with his left keeping the lance raised, says:

"I, priest and king, take thee, woman, pure without spot; I upraise thee; I set thee upon the summit of the earth."

He enthrones the "priestess" on the altar.

She takes the book and holds it open on her chest. The "priest" gives the lance to the deacon, and makes five crosses upon the "priestess'" forehead, shoulders and waist. The "priest" then kneels in adoration, and says:

"Not unto Thee may we attain unless Thine image be love. Therefore, by seed and root, and stem, and bud, and leaf, and flower, and fruit do we invoke Thee."

During this speech, the "priestess" divests herself completely of her robe.

She speaks:

"But to love is better than all things; if under the night stars in the desert thou presently burnest mine incense before me, invoking me with a pure heart, and the serpent flame therein, thou shalt come a little to abide in my mind.

"For one kiss wilt thou then be willing to give all; but whoso gives one particle of dust shall lose all in that hour.

"Ye shall gather goods and store of women and spices; ye shall wear rich jewels; ye shall exceed the nations of earth in splendor and pride; but always in love.

"I charge you earnestly to come before me in a single robe, and covered with a rich head-dress. I love you! Pale or purple, veiled or unveiled, I am beauty of the innermost sense.

"Put on wings! Sing the rapturous lovesong unto me. Burn to me perfumes. Drink to me, for I love you! I love you! I am the blue-lidded daughter of sunset; I am the brilliance of the night-sky! To me! To me!"

The "priest" approaches nearer and says:

"I am the flame that burns in the heart of every man, and in the core of every star."

The "priestess" says:

"There is no law beyond, Do what thou wilt."

The "priest" parts the veil over the "holy of holies" with his lance, and pronounces in Greek an invocation to the "great God Pan," as the pagan symbol of life.

He presents the lance to the "priestess," who kisses it eleven times. She then holds it to her chest, while the "priest" falls at her knees.

This completes the first part of the ceremony, which is called the Opening of the Veil.

There follows a short ritual.

Next comes the "Consecration of the Elements," the cup of wine and the water. The "priest" touches the latter with the lance, and says:

> *By the virtue of the Rod*
> *Be this wine the Blood of God."*

The "priest" says:

"Life of man upon earth, fruit of labor, sustenance of endeavor, thus be thou nourishment of the spirit."

He elevates the wafer and the cup. The bell strikes. He replaces the wafer and the cup.

The concluding ceremony is called the "Mystic Marriage and Consummation of the Elements." The "priest" holds the wafer. The "priestess" clasps the cup. He says:

"Lord, most, secret, bless this spiritual food unto our bodies, bestowing upon us health and wealth, and strength, and joy and peace, and that fulfilment of will and of love under will that is perpetual happiness."

He uncovers the cup, and breaks a part of the wafer over the cup. The other part is placed upon the point of the lance. The "priest" then clasps the cup in his left hand, and he and the "priestess" together dip the point of the lance into the cup.

The "priest" then turns to the people, lowers and raises the lance, and says.

"Do what thou wilt shall be the whole of the law." The people reply:

"Love is the law, love under will."

The "priestess" then offers the cup from which the "priest" drinks. The people then advance, one by one, to the altar, and partake.

In conclusion, the "priest" says:

"The Lord bring you to the accomplishment of your true wills, true wisdom and perfect happiness."

I am not presenting this ritual to you with my approval, but as recorded fact, exactly as it is—a part of the current history of this man's amazing activities and curious beliefs.

Crowley believes that love should not be regarded as a secret thing, to be whispered about and hidden. He believes that the highest and most complete morality will only come from accepting it as simply as any other essential fact about life. His real views, as he has expressed them to me on this subject—and I can't help it if I irritate him by saying so—are not essentially different from those held by many more "respectable" reformers, for example, H.G. Wells.

An American magazine has published a serial story by Mr. Wells in which he pictures an imaginary Utopia, where all the men and women go without clothes, with practically no laws and no restrictions save their own consciences and wills. Mr. Wells presents these people as actually more moral and happier than they are in the present state of society. That is really the final idea that Crowley has. Not a state of universal license and debauchery, but one in which proper actions come not from compulsion and restraint, but from complete knowledge and the development of the individual will.

The "Do What Thou Wilt" doctrine is not quite so easy to explain, but the central point is that he emphasizes the "will" part of it rather than the mere "doing as you please." He believes that every man and woman, above all else, should try to fulfil his or her own individual destiny by discovering what he or she really wants to do with life, what they really "will" to do, and should then take this as the highest guide and be absolutely true to it.

Strangely enough, he has exactly the same condemnation and denunciation that a reformer would have for people who allow their wills to be led by their appetites. The essential difference is that the reformer believes in escaping these appetites by either shunning or stifling them. Crowley wants to accept them all as a part of life and teach the will to control them—to use them rather than abuse them. It is basically the difference, say Crowley's admirers, between prohibition and temperance.

I am tempted to venture a personal comment though I meant to refrain from it. I think there is a bad flaw in Crowley's doctrine. I personally have told him so many times. And I think this is demonstrated by the rows, scandals and abuses which followed the teaching of his doctrine in Detroit. The flaw, I think, is this:

If all people were strong-willed enough and intelligent enough to live up to such a doctrine, it might be splendid, and perhaps even a beautiful thing for humanity. But the majority of people are neither strong-willed nor intelligent enough. They need restraining influences from the outside. They must have laws and compulsions to make them do right. For them, any such doctrine as "do what thou wilt" simply means unlimited license for debauchery and moral anarchy. If you substitute Will in place of God, then you must have a godlike will—and I think the human will is far from being developed, or promising to develop, to that point, except in the rarest individuals.

Of course, all his experiments haven't turned out so tragically as the fiasco in Detroit. There is the "abbey" in Cefalu, Sicily, the most peculiar colony ever established in modern times, consisting of men, women, and children, all living together under no law except "Do What Thou Wilt" in a big villa and grounds on a mountainside overlooking the Mediterranean.

I have in my possession letters, diaries, and statement, from a number of persons in the colony, in addition to Crowley himself.

Some of the stuff they contain is so fantastic as to be almost unbelievable. I shall tell about it in the next chapter.

CHAPTER X.

"WHAT is it really like in Thelema?" I recently cabled Aleister Crowley. He sent me in replying a big package of letters, photographs, diaries and notebooks, which vividly reflect the present daily life of this amazing colony he has established in his "abbey" on the shores of the Mediterranean.

It is a daring experiment—which has been going on now for more than three years—in the practical application of his brazen "Do What Thou Wilt" religion—a little community of men, women and children who have voluntarily isolated themselves from the conventional life and the conventional code of modern civilization, to try to live in "an entirely new way."

The place itself, though Crowley calls it "The Abbey of Thelema," is in reality an old Italian villa on a country hillside, immediately overlooking the sea, not far from Palermo, and just above the medieval town of Cefalu, in Sicily.

The hill itself is close to a great rocky promontory, whose pinnacles tower above it, and on which are the ruins of old Greek temples and Roman walls.

Housed in this villa and on its surrounding grounds is the small community of which Crowley is the head.

They dress, eat, act, think differently from any people you have ever known. Their lives, to the average conventional person, are as fantastic as the lives of people on another planet described by

H.G. Wells.

Absolute freedom, but a freedom achieved by fearless iconoclasm and complete development of the will-power and confidence in the supremacy of their own convictions—this is the basis of Crowley's cult.

His idea is that abso-essential evil—that the evil of anything is only in its misuse. He claims to have cured people of the drug habit. He claims to be teaching them a higher love morality. Yet if you went to this abbey you would find opium, cocaine, hasheesh lying around as freely as butter and eggs; you would quite likely encounter beautiful girls, if the weather happened to be warm, sunning themselves or going about their affairs as unconscious of their nudity as so many household pets.

Yet not only Crowley himself, but other persons who write to me about this "abbey," tell me that even by conventional standards of morality what actually goes on there is no more wicked than the usual life of an average city, where people go clothed, drugs are banned, a thousand laws are in operation and policemen on every corner.

Included in the first-hand information I have obtained from this "abbey" is a mass of notes from an American girl, Jane Wolfe, formerly an actress and motion picture scenario writer in Los Angeles. I don't know why she first went there to become a member of Crowley's community. It may be that she was tired of a "prohibition" country and wanted to go to a place where there were no "prohibitions"—to another extreme, where "Do What Thou Wilt" was the only law. Maybe she thought it meant complete freedom to do as she pleased.

Judging from the notes and letters she has sent me she must have suffered a considerable shock. "It is all right to do your will," Crowley told her, "but first of all, you must discover what your REAL will is, and then train it to obey you."

In order to help her discover her "true will" Crowley made her retire alone to one of the adjacent rocky crags, with no bed but a blanket and no covering but an inadequate "pup-tent," where she had to remain for thirty days engaged in contemplation and self-study. During the greater part of this time she had to sit on the rock, in a cramped, motionless position, like a Buddhist monk, exposed not only to the sun and rain, but also to the gaze of any members of the community who might happen to be passing.

This final detail was "to accustom her to the essential dignity of the human body and the absolute unimportance of whether it is clothed or not."

She had a terrible time during the first part of her "retirement" to discover her "true will." She was even stoned by mischievous Italian boys from a neighboring village. She tells all about it in a diary which she kept from day to day. But she stuck it out and at the end of thirty days joined the community. That was two years ago. She has been there ever since. She thinks she has discovered her "true will." It happens to be the desire to write. So she stays there and writes and, she says, lives a life of absolute freedom.

The chief permanent residents of the "abbey" today are ten persons—five men, three women and two children. Crowley has tabulated the adults to me in his characteristic, methodical way:

Nationality	Social Status	Profession
1. English	Old country family	Poet and philosopher
2. Swiss-American	Middle class with infiltration of French nobility	Teacher in public schools in U.S.A. and director
3. French	Southern peasant stock	Nurse
4. American	Pennsylvania Dutch middle class	Actress
5. American	New England stock	Naval hospital attendant
6. English	Wessex aristocracy	Writer
7. Scotch	Scotch ancient nobility	Writer, soldier and civil servant
8. English	Lancaster working class	Carpenter

In the "abbey" of Thelema these people take new names, mostly classical or pagan appellations. The women are called Athena, Cypris, Lala; the men Lamus, Dionysus, etc. Crowley says he doesn't attach any special importance to the changing of the names, except that it helps the individuals to get away from their old "Benighted" selves.

Those who have been following these articles will recognize as No. 1 Crowley himself. They will recognize in No. 2 Lea Hirsig, the Swiss-American girl, first known as "The Dead Soul" and afterward as "The Scarlet Woman," who went abroad with Crowley. No. 3 is a French girl by the name of Ninette Frank who has never been to America. Crowley found her, I believe, in Paris. No. 4 is Jane Wolfe, the American girl from Los Angeles, about whom I told you above.

The two children in the community are Howard, five years old, son of Ninette Frank, and Hansi, three and a half, son of the "Dead Soul."

In Thelema each individual wears a single short garment, a robe or shirt—or, as he chooses, nothing at all. The food is wholesome, but always of a kind that can be most quickly prepared and the scraps easily cleaned away. The furniture, too, is reduced to the simplest equations. The beds are couches. In short, everything is reduced to the economy of a perpetual "camping trip." The "abbey's" occupants like comfort. They enjoy luxuries. But both must be of a sort that do not get in their way and take up too much time.

What us the sense in living this way, instead of more elaborately as most people do? Maybe no sense at all for you or for me. But this is the way Jane Wolfe justifies it:

"In civilized life, so-called, at least two-thirds of every one's time is wasted on things that don't matter. The idea of this place is to give every one the maximum time for doing his own will. When I came here two years ago every detail was an annoyance and an insult. Also, I was bored. There is absolutely nothing to do here in the way of amusement. The housework occupies practically no time at all because of its simplification. There is nowhere to go. The result is that with eating and everything else thrown in there is not much more than an hour of our waking time occupied by what one may call necessary work.

"Compare that with life in New York, or any other city. Mere dressing in conventional society takes up more time than that. With the simple garments we wear here, to dress or undress is a matter of three seconds, and these robes are practical for everything but rock-climbing. Even our climbing clothes—consisting of only shirts, breeches and tennis shoes—require but three or four minutes to change.

"In a city, if we are bored we look around for some diversion; we chatter, go to a theatre or movie, play cards—kill time without solving the real problem of our boredom—we only dodge it. But here there are no such diversions. One has to be very stupid not to discover within forty-eight hours that there is no possibility of amusing oneself in any of the ordinary ways. So one finds oneself up against the fact that one has to discover something to do. We go to Crowley and say, 'What shall we do?' He says, 'Do what thou wilt.'

"'Yes,' we say, 'but what is that?'

"'How should I know?' he replies rudely. 'Go and find out.'

"'Examine yourself,' he says. 'Examine your faculties and tendencies, the trend of your mind and the aspirations of your soul. Allow me to assure you that you will find this investigation leaves you very little time to wonder what to do for amusement.'

"In other words, Crowley uses the same method as the old mystical societies, which shut up candidates for initiation in silence and darkness. They had the choice between going mad or turning their minds inward and learning to study and know themselves.

"It is only after discovering what our true will really is that we begin to practice it. And once discovered, it makes no difference what it is, so long as it is true self-expression. It may be writing or painting. It may be working in a blacksmith shop or breaking rock. It may be hard manual labor. It may be sitting in contemplation and doing absolutely nothing.

"In dealing with so-called indulgences, Crowley believes in conquering them just as truly as any schoolmaster. But his method is totally different. The latter wants you to let your indulgences alone. Crowley wants you to learn by experience what they really are, and to have not merely the power to use, and even enjoy, them, too, without succumbing to them. The teacher wants you to say 'No' to all such things. Crowley wants you to be able to say 'Yes' or 'No,' indifferently and without fear, to all physical things."

"What a place for little children!" you are thinking, and wondering how those two baby boys, Howard and Hansi, are being brought up in such an extraordinary community. Well, I haven't any word direct from Howard or Hansi on the subject. They are too young to write and express themselves. But their mothers think they are "developing marvelously." As to the final results of this amazing child-training, no one knows what its outcome will be, but exactly what this training consists of, Crowley explained to me freely in a recent letter.

The basis of it, of course, is, "Do what thou wilt." Crowley applied his creed even to children. How would you like to try it on children of your own? From the time they could think for themselves, Howard and Hansi were permitted to do exactly what they wanted. If Hansi wanted the brandy bottle instead of the milk bottle, they let him have it. They let him make himself ill, and then carefully explained why it had made him ill, and told him if he liked being ill to help himself again. He decided not to. They didn't remove the bottle from his reach. But he didn't touch it any more.

If Howard wanted to touch a hot stove with his fingers they let him touch it, and they explained why it hurt him. They didn't remove the stove or forbid him to go near it. "You know how it works now," they told him. "If it is your will not to be burned, stay away from it."

But let Crowley speak for himself about the "education" of these children. He says:

"Each child must develop its own peculiar individuality and will, disregarding all other ideas or ideals. Here its natural resources and originality are matched against its environment. It is confronted with such problems as swimming, climbing, housework, and permitted to solve them in its own way. Nothing can be really taught a child except how to think for itself. Here it is treated as a responsible, independent being, encouraged in self-reliance and respected for self-assertion.

"True education is simply assisting a soul to express itself. Every child should be presented with all possible problems and permitted to register its own reactions. Its mind must not be influenced, but only offered all kinds of nourishment. Its innate qualities will enable it to select the things proper for its nature. Respect the child's individuality! Submit all life for its inspection, but without comment. Freedom develops will; experience gives resourcefulness; independence inspires self-confidence.

"Those who train children according to fixed standards cripple and deform them.

Every child is a sphinx, and none knows its secret but itself. Every child is the god of its own universe and must be taught nothing but to govern its environment."

If you haven't been reading this series of articles, you may think, from this chapter alone, that I am writing a defense of Crowley—that I am trying to impose his ideas upon you. That is not so. I repeat that I am neither attacking nor defending Crowley. I am chronicling him as I knew him—the good and bad—all of it.

Last week I told you in detail of the scandal that followed the establishment of a chapter of his cult in Detroit. In an earlier chapter I quoted attacks on his "abbey" made by a London newspaper. And it is only fair in this chapter that I present another side—the "abbey" as he sees it himself and as the "disciples" see it.

Next week I shall describe the excitement which prevailed in London when it became known that one of Crowley's "disciples," Raoul Loveday, a young Englishman, had died at Crowley's "abbey."

For the sake of justice, I shall give first the dramatically vivid account by the "disciples'" window of activities at the "abbey," and then quote from one of Crowley's letters referring to the same set of circumstances.

CHAPTER XI.

THE LONDON *DAILY EXPRESS*, which has been conducting a series of startling attacks on Aleister Crowley, recently publishing the story of a "beautiful young wife," who told of "unspeakable orgies" at Crowley's "holy abbey" in Cefalu, Sicily. She described how her young husband died there, in dreadful circumstances, after he had come under the influence of the "Beast."

The story was printed anonymously. The names and identities of the young widow and her dead husband were carefully concealed by the *Daily Express*.

The statement of the girl has been reproduced in several American newspapers, still with the names and essential details left out.

Here, for the first time, are the extraordinary facts:

The husband, who died at Crowley's "abbey" after becoming his disciple, was Raoul Loveday, a brilliant graduate of Oxford University, a deep student of mysticism and a member of a well-known English family.

The young widow, whose denunciations of Crowley and his colony the *Express* published, is Betty May Loveday, who was an artists' model in London prior to her marriage.

Despite the sensational accusations thrown over this affair, Loveday died a natural death, from enteritis (inflammation of the intestines), with a physician in attendance.

I have these facts, not from Crowley, but from sources in England which I believe are dispassionate and just. The circumstances of the death were attested by the Italian municipal authorities, just as required in American cities, and the records are on file.

I have, also, however, a long letter from Crowley himself, in which he comments on Betty Loveday's story, frankly admitting many of the things she charges, but declaring that others are "cruelly distorted in some instances and absolutely untrue in others."

Here is part of what Betty Loveday says about the experiences of herself and her husband when they became members of Crowley's extraordinary colony:

"We reached Cefalu. Our reception was startling. The door was opened by a woman whom we were to know later as Jane (Jane Wolfe, of Los Angeles, one of the American girls who joined Crowley's colony).

"'Beast,' she cried out, 'here are Mr. and Mrs. ———.'

"Crowley appeared. He raised one hand above his head and said, 'Do what thou wilt shall be the whole of the law.'

"To this I heard half a dozen other voices reply, 'Love is the law; love under will.'

"As a general rule, Crowley is not seen by anyone before teatime. He remains in his own room, 'Cauchemar,' or 'Nightmare,' as it is called—drugging himself. His room is full of drugs of all sorts: there is a great bottle of raw hasheesh and bottles of cocaine, heroin, morphia and ether. He distils his own opium, a lot of which is smoked in the 'abbey.' You can have whatever dope you like by asking for it.

"At four o'clock my husband and I were summoned to 'Cauchemar.' Crowley received us lying on his bed, his totally bald head covered with a black wig. (At certain periods Crowley shaves his head like a

Buddhist monk.) He gave us our instructions. He named me 'Sister Sibyline' and instructed me to do the cooking and keep the house clean. My husband, for the present, was to play chess and read with the 'Beast.'

"Once a day every one in the colony must come inside the 'magic circle.' At 7:30 we all trooped into the temple where the circle is marked on the floor. A great charcoal fire burns in the center. The 'Beast's' chair stands on the north side of the circle, with a brazier in front of him and six colored receptacles for his swords and magic wands. I refused to sit inside the circle and was allowed to remain outside. Incense was burned before Crowley, who was robed in scarlet and wearing magnificent rings. Lea (Lea Hirsig, former New York school teacher), known here at the 'Scarlet Woman,' Crowley's companion and high priestess, was clad in a red robe edged with gold. All the trappings were of indescribable richness.

"The days went on. My husband was initiated into Crowley's mystic cult of the O.T.O., but he would never tell me about the ceremony. All I know is that he wore gorgeous robes, that the ceremony lasted eight hours, and that he was presented with a book, for which he was supposed to pay.

"Now I come to the sickening episode of the cat. At tea one afternoon Crowley was in a peculiar mood, irritable and uneasy. Suddenly he arose and said, 'There is an evil spirit here.' He noticed a cat in the room. 'Within three day,' the 'Beast' ordained, 'that cat must be sacrificed.' Then a very remarkable thing happened. As a rule, the cat would run away if anyone came near it; but Crowley approached it and made passes over it with his magic sword and the cat never moved.

"The third day arrived. I wanted to get the cat away, but my husband would not let me interfere. Crowley had told my husband that he must kill the cat. The hour arrived. Above the altar hung a bell formed of an almost flat metal disc, the striker being a human bone. A bowl to catch the cat's blood stood at the side.

"My husband, trembling from head to foot, stood by the altar, armed with a sharp, curved sword. He had to lift the cat in one hand and kill it with the other. The cat struggled violently. Crowley dabbed its nose with ether until it became quiet.

"The reading of a long invocation was concluded. 'Now,' said the 'Beast.' My husband struck at the wretched animal, but only half-killed it. He had to pick it up again, and finally, with a hard blow, severed its head from its body. Jane hid the body of the cat, which happened to belong to a neighbor, and threw it into the sea the following day.

"Other incidents and practices indulged in at the 'abbey' it is impossible to describe. With every day my horror and repulsion grew."

Mrs. Loveday tells next how her husband fell ill "from eating too many oranges," and how she had a quarrel with Crowley which resulted in his ordering her out of the "abbey." She went down to the little town of Cefalu, where she got a note from her husband saying he was worse.

"I rushed back to the 'abbey.' I saw my husband. He looked dreadfully bad. 'What is it, darling?' I asked.

"'Ask Crowley to let you come back,' he said.

"I looked at his pale, wan face and didn't wait to ask. I stayed. "Meanwhile the doctor had visited my husband and had gone away promising to send some medicine. But the medicine did not come until too late. I was desperate and hardly knew what to do.

"'Are you comfortable dear?' I asked him.

"'Yes. I do love you, darling; I do.'

"These were the last words my husband ever spoke to me. To my amazement I was asked to go down into the town to buy an article for the sickroom. When I returned the woman, Jane, stood in the doorway.

"'He's gone,' she said.

"'Where?' I asked.

"'He's dead,' she replied.

"I remember nothing until six o'clock—two hours later. It is a regulation of the civic authorities in Cefalu that no dead body may remain in a private house after 7 p.m.

"They tried in vain to keep me from the funeral. Then I rushed to Cefalu. I must somehow or other send a telegram. But I had no money. While I was trying, in dumbshow, to persuade the postmaster to send one, a telegram form Palermo arrived for me. It was in reply to a letter I had sent the British Consul, and he was sending me fifty lire so I could go to him.

"I flew back to the 'abbey.' Escape was my one thought. Crowley, who had never paid me the slightest attention up to this time and rarely ever spoke to me or noticed my existence, said, 'You will make this your home; you have no money.'

"'I am going back to England,' I replied. 'I have money. The British Consul has sent me fifty lire.'

"'Jane is going to London shortly,' he retorted. 'You will be back here in three months.' I turned and ran for the door. The 'Beast' saw I was going. He laid one finger on his lips and said, in a tone half advice and half menace.

"'Silence, you understand?'

"The British Consul at Palermo sent me home to England."

How does it happen that this young woman consented to go to Sicily at all and become one of the colony? The truth—which I have learned from people who knew her in London—is that she didn't willingly consent. She went only because her husband insisted.

This husband, young Loveday, was the person in whom Crowley was really interested in having as a member of the colony. The wife was only an incident. Loveday, like Crowley himself, was an ardent and serious student of mysticism.

Some of Crowley's poetry young Loveday had read in the *Oxford Book of Mystical Verse*, a standard work published by the university itself and bearing its stamp of literary approval. In addition Crowley had just written a novel, *The Diary of a Drug Fiend*, issued by one of the biggest London publishers, which was making a tremendous sensation.

Young Loveday, therefore, went to Cefalu to learn more about mysticism. And Crowley saw in him a promising disciple who might carry on his work, which, as Crowley sees it, is to teach people to become supermen.

On the subject of young Loveday's death and the things said about the "abbey," Crowley has written me a letter, from which I will quote two paragraphs. Why? Well, I am still trying to give you a full-length portrait of this strange man, goodness and badness mixed.

"Much of what I have done has been indiscreet," wrote Crowley, "and the result is that even many people who are more or less open-minded have supposed me to be a mere voluptuary and debauchee. I can hardly blame them. My best defense, is the quantity of work which I have produced— and the fact that I am trying, without hope of reward, to make something stronger and finer of humanity. You know how intense and passionate is my devotion to that idea. I remember, in America, you told me I ought

not to insist on trying to be a 'messiah'—
that I should give up trying to 'convert'
people and devote my time to poetry. But I
can't help it, for I AM a 'messiah.' You can
call it a delusion, if you please, but if so, it is
a genuine delusion and not a pose.

"The unfortunate thing is that my ideas
are so easily distorted and misunderstood.
This is where the death of Raoul is such a
heavy loss. Before meeting me he had put
in two years and more of solid work in
studying. He had the elements at the tips of
his fingers, so that from the first I was able
to make myself understood. In three years I
could have made him the most brilliant and
learned exponent that heart could desire."

Perhaps you will remember, if you have
been reading this true-to-life serial, that in
the opening chapters I told you there were
people who regard Crowley as a beast and
monster and madman—and others who
regarded him as a poet and moralist and genius. I think, in this chapter, you can find a
little of most of those things, for, mind you,
a great deal of the fantastic stuff told by Mrs.
Loveday of what she saw at the "abbey" is
literally true, on Crowley's own admission.

That Crowley or his "witchcraft" had
anything to do with the death of Raoul

Loveday—as some sensational British newspapers are hinting—is flatly impossible. But that Crowley has incense burned before him, did cause an unhappy stray cat to be killed under the impression it was an evil spirit, I think is quite likely, for it is thoroughly in keeping with the practices of "Black Magic" in which he believes.

These practices would naturally strike anyone not in sympathy with Aleister Crowley's "magical" philosophy as wild, distorted, fantastic and even, in certain extraordinary circumstances, as perhaps malign and demonic.

Mrs. Loveday, for example, seems to have looked on the incidents that preceded and followed her husband's death as extraordinary and terrible; and to her mind, they undoubtedly were. But that the ritual of the "O.T.O." has, or had, anything to do with her husband's illness is simply out of the question. Such a supposition would give the lie to Crowley's passionately affirmed, if peculiarly expressed, "faith in mankind."

In a final chapter I shall tell you of Crowley's experiences in the use of all drugs and his extraordinary methods of trying to "cure" people of the narcotic habit in his "Do What Thou Wilt" abbey.

CHAPTER XII.

WHAT would you think of a sanitarium for drink-victims in which the chief feature was a de luxe bar, stocked with every variety of whiskey, wine and beer, where the patients—as well as the doctors and nurses—were permitted to drink as much as they pleased and whenever they pleased?

Sounds like the idea of a crazy man, doesn't it? Well, that is precisely the kind of a "drug-cure" Aleister Crowley has set up in his strange colony at Cefalu, Sicily, where Lea, the "Scarlet Woman," Jane Wolfe, the former movie star, and other men and women—some university graduates and some day laborers from the field—venerate him as the teacher of a "new morality," the prophet of a new aeon, and as the "Beast of the Apocalypse," whose coming is foretold in the Bible.

I have the facts, directly and personally, from persons who have visited the place. Besides, Crowley himself admits them in a letter to me, and says, "Go ahead and tell all about it if you want to; I have nothing to conceal."

Maybe nothing to conceal in Sicily. But if he were in America he would have "something to conceal," all right, for in his "abbey" there is a pantry shelf, on which are stored quantities of every imaginable narcotic drug—bottles of cocaine, heroin and morphine, boxes and tins of opium, cans of ether, distillations of hasheesh—all as easy of access as the butter and eggs and milk in your ice box.

Fantastic, crazy, illogical, you think? I think so, too. And the most fantastic, crazy, illogical feature is that in some individual cases, at least, it apparently has worked. It has effected cures where orthodox methods have failed, Crowley claims.

When all is said and done, the chief world-wide interest in Crowley at this moment, particularly in England and America, centers in the sensation made by his book, *The Diary of a Drug Fiend*. It is a novel about cocaine, heroin, morphine and opium—a true story, in which the characters and places are thinly distinguished under a veil of fiction.

Crowley paints in detail the delirious ecstasies of the drug user's false paradise in the earlier stages of addiction.

Later he depicts the horrors and tortures of the victim, bound hand and foot by the habit he cannot break.

Finally Crowley describes his own amazing methods of so-called "cure" and his extraordinary colony in the south of Italy.

He believes, like the orthodox reformers, and, indeed, like all sane human beings, that drug addiction is a terrible curse—but there is nothing orthodox about his ideas of how humanity shall get rid of it!

Here are some of the passages which aroused the wrath of reformers in England and on which they based their demand for the suppression of the book. The publishers defended themselves successfully by quoting other passages which depict, in even more vivid language, the horrors and evils of the same drugs.

Describing the "paradise of cocaine," Crowley writes:

"Until you've got your mouth full of cocaine, you don't know what kissing is. One kiss goes on from phase to phase like a novel by Balzac or Zola. And you never get tired. You're on fourth speed all the time, and the engine purrs like a kitten—a big white kitten with the stars in its whiskers. And it's always different, and always the same, and it never stops, and you go insane, and you stay insane, and you probably don't know what I'm talking about, and I don't care a bit, though I'm awfully sorry for you, and you can find out any minute you like by the simple process of getting a sweetheart like mine and a lot of cocaine."

Of the wholly different first-effects of heroin he writes:

"The heroin began to take hold. We found ourselves crowned with colossal calm. We dressed to go out with, I imagine, the sort of feeling a newly made bishop would have the first time he put on his vestments.

"When we went downstairs we felt like gods descending upon earth—immeasurably beyond mortality. We were dignified beyond all words to express. Our voices sounded far, far off. We were convinced that the hotel porter realized he was receiving the order of Jupiter and Juno to get a taxi.

We never doubted that the chauffeur knew himself to be the charioteer of the gods.

"As we drove toward the Sacre Coeur, we remained completely silent, lost in the calm beatitude. Instead of beating passionately up the sky with flaming wings, we were poised aloft in the illimitable ether. We took fresh doses of the dull, soft powder now and again. We did so without greed, hurry or even desire. The sensation was of infinite power which could afford infinite deliberation. Will itself seemed to have been abolished. We were going nowhere in particular, simply because it was our nature to do so. Our beatitude became more absolute every moment.

"With cocaine one feels oneself master of everything; but everything matters intensely. With heroin, the feeling of mastery increases to such a point that nothing matters at all."

Pretty nice, eh? Like to try it yourself, perhaps if you knew where you could get some dope? Well, just read on a bit before you go out looking for a peddler, and maybe it won't seem quite so nice. Here's what the same man says about the cost of entering this false paradise—and this is true stuff mind you, from the actual experience, this time of a highly bred, beautiful and intelligent English girl who became a cocaine and heroin victim.

"I wanted now to stop heroin and cocaine, to fight them to a finish, but my hands were tied behind my back, my feet were fettered by a chain and ball.

"P—— (the girl's husband, also a victim) had gone to sleep. He snored and groaned. He was like one's idea of a convict. He hadn't shaved for two days. My own nails were black. I felt sticky and clammy all over. I went to the looking-glass. I didn't know who I was. My complexion is entirely gone. My hair is lusterless and dry, and it's coming out in handfuls. I think I must be ill. I've got a good mind to send for a doctor. But I daren't.

"We have both had spasms of weakness, a ghastly sensation of the sinking of the spirit. It is the same dread that seizes one in an elevator that starts down too quickly. Waves of weakness washed over us as if we were corpses cast up by the sea from a shipwreck. A shipwreck of our souls. And in these hideous hours of helplessness we drifted down the dark and sluggish river of inertia toward the stagnant, loathsome morass of insanity. We were obsessed by the certainty that we could never pull through. It must be so, that we couldn't pull through, because the doctors, reformers, vice-crusaders, everybody said so. We were sunk in a stupor. When we found voice at last, it was to whimper our surrender. The unconditional surrender of our integrity and honor. And on top of everything else was the torture of shame, for I had always been proud of my pride.

"I wonder how I have lived through this. When P—— came home last night I had never seen him like it before. His eyes were half out of his head, bloodshot and furious. Unable to get drugs, he had been drinking like a madman. He came straight up to me and hit me deliberately in the face. He staggered back into the middle of the room and pointed to the blood that was running down my face. The edge of his ring had cut the corner of my eye. The sight sent him into fits of hysterical laughter.

"I burst out crying. The contrast with what had been was too shocking. I had married a fine, courteous English gentleman, and drugs had turned him into this screaming, swearing bully, with his insane jealousy and senseless brutality.

"He staggered and groped his way round the room looking for me. He stumbled up against me, gripped me by the shoulder, and began to strike. I sat as if I were paralyzed. I couldn't even scream. He swore and struck at me savagely, yet now so weakly that I could not feel the blows. Besides, I think I was dulled to pain.

"Presently he collapsed and rolled over on the bed. I thought for a moment he was dead, and then he was seized by a series of spasms; his muscles twisted and twitched; his hands clawed at the air; he began to mutter rapidly. I was horribly frightened.

"I got up and lit the gas. The poor boy's face was white as death, but small, dark, crimson flushes burnt on the cheek bones. I didn't dare send for a doctor. He might know what was the matter with both of us. Presently P—— went to sleep.

"A dreadful thing happened. We had used up all the heroin and cocaine, and couldn't get any more. I remembered that once before I had sewn some little cloth packets of heroin in the lining of my white frock, and went to get it. We had been living without servants, like pigs, and it was on the floor, in the corner of the drawing room.

"It was all shrunk and rumpled and dirty, and it was still quite wet. I suppose

I must have gone out in the rain, though I don't remember anything about it.

"All the heroin was washed away. There wasn't a grain left. P——, too, had wanted some dreadfully; finding it gone made him want it insanely.

"He took one of the packets and began to chew it. 'Thank God,' he said. 'It's quite bitter. There must be a lot in the dress.'

"I was shivering and faint. I got another packet and put it in my mouth. He went wild and clutched me by the hair and forced open my jaws with his finger and thumb. I struggled and kicked and scratched, but he was too strong. He got the heroin out of my mouth and put it in his own mouth. I went flat and limp and began to cry.

"He picked up the dress and packets and started to go. I caught at his ankles desperately, but he kicked himself free and went out of the room with the dress.

"I feel that I shall scream if this goes on much longer; and by scream I don't mean just an ordinary scream; I mean that I shall scream and scream and scream and never stop.

"I am conscious of nothing but this tearing, stabbing, gnawing pain; this restless, raging, trembling of the body; this malignant tearing of the open wound of my soul."

Crowley got this unhappy girl and her husband down to his "abbey" in Cefalu, and undertook to cure them.

Don't ask me if I think there is anything in this method of "cure." I don't know. I am not advocating it. I am merely quoting. For the normal, sensible human being the only safe method of dealing with dope is to let it absolutely and completely alone.

Since the publication of this series of articles began I have received letters and communications about Aleister Crowley from every quarter of the globe—even from Australia and Tierra del Fuego. They are mostly from people of whom I never heard. To quote them all would require a book. Some of them picture Crowley as a holy man, a saint, sacrificing himself to teach humanity a new religion of freedom; others depict him as a monster of depravity, hypocrisy and dishonesty.

What is the real truth about this extraordinary character? I don't think you can have discovered it from reading these chapters, for I confess that I don't pretend to have discovered it in writing them. I have known Crowley for years. I own most of his books.

I have a mass of material written about him, both by his friends and enemies. Yet he remains an enigma.

Once in talking with me about his long Asiatic travels, he said: "When you read or hear any stories about the interior of China, no matter how incredible they may happen to be, it is never safe to take for granted they are lies. No matter how fantastic the story may be; no matter how cruel, how impossibly wicked and vile on the one hand, or how beautiful and saintlike and holy it may be on the other—there is always the possibility that somewhere in that great, mysterious interior of China the story may be true."

I've often thought of that statement in connection with Aleister Crowley, and have wondered if he wasn't unconsciously drawing a picture of himself as well as of the Mysterious East.